250

"Thank You, Honey, For Giving Me The Most Precious Gift A Woman Can Give A Man—His Child."

"I should be thanking you," Kaylee said softly. "Amber is the best thing that's ever happened to me. From the moment I suspected I was pregnant with her, I was thrilled."

Her quiet statement seemed to rob him of breath. All things considered, most women would have been fit to be tied by an unexpected pregnancy. "Why, Kaylee?" Colt asked. "Why were you happy at the prospect of having a baby?"

She leaned back to stare up at him. "Because I knew the baby was a part of you," she whispered.

Colt's heart stalled, then took off at a dead run. Kaylee had welcomed his child, loved and nurtured her, even before she'd known for sure that Amber was growing in her belly. He had a hard time expressing how much her admission meant to him. Groaning, he simply lowered his mouth to hers, letting her know without words what he was feeling.

He'd told her they would allow their feelings to build before they took the next step in their relationship. But it had been three long years since he'd made love to her, and the need to once again make Kaylee his clouded his mind. Taking things slowly was no longer an option for them, and as she melted against him, Colt wasn't sure that it had ever been.

Dear Reader,

Thanks for choosing Silhouette Desire, where we bring you the ultimate in powerful, passionate and provocative love stories. Our immensely popular series DYNASTIES: THE BARONES comes to a rollicking conclusion this month with Metsy Hingle's *Passionately Ever After*. But don't worry, another wonderful family saga is on the horizon. Come back next month when Barbara McCauley launches DYNASTIES: THE DANFORTHS. Full of Southern charm—and sultry scandals—this is a series not to be missed!

The wonderful Dixie Browning is back with an immersing tale in *Social Graces*. And Brenda Jackson treats readers to another unforgettable—and unbelievably hot!—hero in *Thorn's Challenge*. Kathie DeNosky continues her trilogy about hard-to-tame men with the fabulous *Lonetree Ranchers: Colt*.

Also this month is another exciting installment in the TEXAS CATTLEMAN'S CLUB: THE STOLEN BABY series. Laura Wright pens a powerful story with *Locked Up With a Lawman*—I think the title says it all. And welcome back author Susan Crosby who kicks off her brand-new series, BEHIND CLOSED DOORS, with the compelling *Christmas Bonus, Strings Attached*.

With wishes for a happy, healthy holiday season,

Melissa Jeglinski

Melissa Jeglinski
Senior Editor, Silhouette Desire

Please address questions and book requests to:
Silhouette Reader Service
U.S.: 3010 Walden Ave., P.O. Box 1325, Buffalo, NY 14269
Canadian: P.O. Box 609, Fort Erie, Ont. L2A 5X3

Lonetree
Ranchers: Colt
KATHIE
DENOSKY

Published by Silhouette Books
America's Publisher of Contemporary Romance

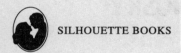

SILHOUETTE BOOKS

ISBN 0-373-76551-7

LONETREE RANCHERS: COLT

Copyright © 2003 by Kathie DeNosky

This edition published by arrangement with Harlequin Books S.A.

® and TM are trademarks of Harlequin Books S.A., used under license. Trademarks indicated with ® are registered in the United States Patent and Trademark Office, the Canadian Trade Marks Office and in other countries.

Visit Silhouette at www.eHarlequin.com

Printed in U.S.A.

Books by Kathie DeNosky

Silhouette Desire

Did You Say Married?! #1296
The Rough and Ready Rancher #1355
His Baby Surprise #1374
Maternally Yours #1418
Cassie's Cowboy Daddy #1439
Cowboy Boss #1457
A Lawman in Her Stocking #1475
In Bed with the Enemy #1521
Lonetree Ranchers: Brant #1528
Lonetree Ranchers: Morgan #1540
Lonetree Ranchers: Colt #1551

Silhouette Books

Home for the Holidays
"New Year's Baby"

KATHIE DeNOSKY

lives in her native southern Illinois with her husband and one very spoiled Jack Russell terrier. She writes highly sensual stories with a generous amount of humor. Kathie's books have appeared on the Waldenbooks best-seller list and received the Write Touch Readers' Award from WisRWA and the National Readers' Choice Award. She enjoys going to rodeos, traveling to research settings for her books and listening to country music. Readers may contact Kathie at P.O. Box 2064, Herrin, Illinois 62948-5264 or e-mail her at kathie@kathiedenosky.com.

To professional bull rider Tater Porter, for taking the
time to answer my many questions and for
sharing his experience and knowledge with me.
Thanks, Tater. You're one of the best.

To Dr. Tandy Freeman and physical trainer
Dave Lammers, for giving me a tour of a
PBR training room and for explaining
how they assist injured riders.

And a special thank-you to the Professional Bull Riders
for showing me a behind-the-scenes look at this exciting
sport. Without their help the Lonetree Ranchers series
would not have been possible.

One

As Kaylee Simpson arranged rolls of gauze and tape on a cart in the training room, the sudden hushed silence of the Ford Center crowd sent a numbing fear straight through her. There was only one reason an arena full of Professional Bull Riders fans became that quiet—one of the riders was down and not moving.

Closing her eyes, she held her breath and tried not to think as she waited for the applause that would signal the rider was being helped to his feet. But with each passing minute the likelihood of that happening dwindled considerably. When she heard several sets of boots hurrying down the corridor to-

ward the training room, she knew they were bringing the rider in on a stretcher.

Dear God, please don't let it be anyone I know,
she prayed.

"Get his vitals," Dr. Carson ordered as he entered the room followed by several other men carrying a stretcher. They hoisted it onto the examining
table.

Grabbing the needed equipment, Kaylee's hands
shook as she stepped up beside the unconscious
cowboy. But the moment she gazed down at the
handsome face of the fallen bull rider, her heart
slammed against her ribs and she felt the blood drain
from her cheeks.

"Colt," she whispered out loud.

The blood pressure cuff fell from her trembling
hands to the floor. She barely noticed.

"You know this guy?" one of the paramedics
asked, picking up the cuff on his way back to the
arena.

Apparently he had no idea who the bull riders
were. But Kaylee knew.

Unable to get words past the huge lump clogging
her throat, she took the cuff from him, closed her
eyes and nodded. She'd grown up around most of
the cowboys on the PBR circuit, and until three
years ago, most of them had been like brothers to
her.

But the one lying on the table in front of her had

always been different. She'd known Colt Wakefield from the time he was sixteen years old and she was ten. He'd been her brother's best friend, the love of her young life and the man who had broken her heart.

"Kaylee, if you're not going to take his blood pressure, step aside and let one of the others do it," Dr. Carson said impatiently as he ran clinical hands over Colt's scalp.

The doctor's sharp tone snapped her out of her shocked state and she moved to follow his directive. Placing the cuff on Colt's arm, she pumped it full of air, then listened with the stethoscope. "His blood pressure is one ten over seventy."

"Good. Help me get his riding gear off and his shirt open so we can see what we have here," Dr. Carson instructed.

Kaylee took a deep breath and unzipped the front of the protective black leather vest with trembling fingers, then released the heavy-duty Velcro closure at Colt's right shoulder while Dr. Carson unfastened the left side. Forcing herself to continue, she pushed the heavy leather out of the way and unsnapped his chambray shirt for the doctor to take a closer look.

But when she parted the garment, the sight of Colt's well-developed chest and rippling stomach muscles sent a shiver straight to her core and brought back memories that she'd worked for three long years to forget. Without thinking, she touched his smooth, warm skin with her fingertips. The last time she'd seen him without a shirt—the last time she'd seen him, period—had been the night after her brother's funeral. Devastated by Mitch's death, they'd turned to each other for comfort and support, and ended up…

"K-Kaylee?"

The sound of Colt's voice caused her to recoil. He'd regained consciousness without her realizing it.

Glancing down into his incredibly blue eyes, she felt as if she might not be able to draw her next breath. "Hi, Colt."

When she'd met him fourteen years ago, she'd decided he was the cutest boy she'd ever seen. But his good looks back then had only been a hint of the devilishly handsome man he would become. With raven hair and brilliant blue eyes, he'd always taken her breath away. Unfortunately, it appeared time hadn't lessened his effect on her.

Deciding to revert to the teasing relationship they'd shared before the events that changed her life forever, she added, "I see you're still doing your famous header dismount."

His lean cheeks flushed a dull red. "And I see you're still the same smart-mouthed little brat you've always been," he said, the mischievous light dancing in his eyes taking the sting from his words.

"That's where you're wrong, cowboy," she said,

smiling sadly. Unable to stop herself, she added, "If you'll remember, I had to grow up pretty fast about three years ago."

Colt felt as if he'd been punched in the gut by Kaylee's cryptic comment. He wasn't sure if she was referring to Mitch's death or how he'd walked away without looking back the morning after the most incredible night of his life. Either way, the guilt that had plagued him for the past three years welled up inside until he felt as if it might choke the life out of him.

"How have you been, Kaylee?" he asked, unsure of what else to say. He watched her tuck a strand of silky auburn hair behind her ear as if trying to figure out how best to answer his question.

"I've survived. I finally finished my degree last year."

He frowned. "What took you so long? A few years ago you only had one more year left."

She seemed to avoid looking directly at him. "Something came up and I had to take time off from school." She wiped the dirt from his face with a damp cloth. "What about you, Colt? How have you been?"

He started to shrug, but the grinding pain in his left shoulder shot up the side of his neck and caused a low groan to echo throughout the training room. Humiliated at having Kaylee see him in such a weakened condition, he gritted his teeth and said the first thing that came to mind. "I'd be a hell of a lot better if you weren't standing over me like a vulture."

As soon as the words were out, Colt cursed himself for being a dirty lowlife snake. He'd rather cut off his right arm than to hurt Kaylee more than he knew he already had. But from the expression that fleetingly crossed her pretty face, he could tell that was exactly what he'd done.

Before he could apologize for being a total jerk, Dr. Carson broke the tension filling the small room. "It looks like you've got a broken collarbone in addition to a slight concussion, Colt. To be sure, I'm sending you to the hospital for a set of X rays."

Colt stared at the man as the gravity of the diagnosis sank in, along with an overwhelming amount of frustrated disappointment. "How long will I be out of commission?"

"Depending on how bad the break is, I'd say you're looking at eight to twelve weeks before you make it back," Carson answered.

It was the very last thing Colt wanted to hear. Ranked number three on this year's PBR tour, he was close enough to the top that he had a damned good shot at the season championship. Missing the last part of the regular season events would all but end his hopes of winning the title. The best he could hope for now was to make it back in time for the finals in November.

"I've called the ambulance crew for transport to the hospital," he heard Kaylee say from somewhere across the room.

She'd made good her escape and had moved away from the examining table while the doctor talked to him. Colt couldn't say that he blamed her. He should be horsewhipped for the way he'd talked to her and he needed to apologize.

"Kaylee?"

A man in a navy-blue paramedic jumpsuit with the name of Forrester embroidered on the breast pocket stepped close. "Are you wanting the cute little chick with the great set of—"

"Watch it, pal," Colt warned angrily. As long as he was around, he wouldn't tolerate anyone talking about Kaylee like that. She deserved the utmost respect and Colt intended to make sure she got it. "That girl just happens to be my best friend's sister."

Knowing Colt was in no shape to do anything about his comment, the man shrugged. "That's funny. She didn't look like much of a girl to me."

Colt ground his back teeth at the guy's lascivious expression. "And just what *did* she look like to you, Forrester?"

"One hundred percent all woman," the man answered, grinning suggestively.

If Colt hadn't been flat on his back and in pain, he'd have knocked the guy into the middle of next week. But as much as he wanted to teach the jerk a lesson in respect, he knew it would be some time before he was up to a good old-fashioned fistfight.

"Don't worry, cowboy. She was on her way out when we came in," the man went on as he and his rotund partner lifted Colt to the gurney they'd rolled up beside the examining table. "She'll most likely meet us at the hospital."

Colt didn't say anything as they transported him out of the training room to the ambulance. He knew damned good and well that Kaylee wouldn't be there when they arrived at the hospital.

After what happened three years ago, combined with the way he'd talked to her this evening, he'd be lucky if she ever spoke to him again.

A month after seeing Colt at the Professional Bull Riders event, Kaylee still found herself thinking about their encounter. He'd been the last person she'd wanted to see. From his reaction, it had been crystal clear that he'd felt the same way about seeing her.

She poured herself a fresh cup of coffee and wandered into the living room of her small apartment to curl up in a corner of the couch. Their run-in had dredged up some painful memories that she thought she'd worked through. Apparently she'd been wrong.

Over the years, cheering for Colt and her brother,

Mitch, had become a tradition. She'd been on hand that fateful weekend three years ago for the PBR event in Houston. But what had started out as a typical Saturday evening of watching the two men she loved most in the world compete in the first round of bull riding had suddenly turned horribly tragic.

Colt had successfully ridden the bull he'd drawn, then helped Mitch pull his rope to get ready for his ride. But the moment the chute gate opened, Kaylee had known Mitch was in serious trouble. The bull's first jump had been violent, whipping Mitch forward and slamming his face into the back of the bull's head, knocking him out. Bullfighters had moved in immediately, but before they could even distract the animal, Mitch had landed on the ground in front of the angry beast.

Tears welled in Kaylee's eyes as she relived the horrific events. The bullfighters had distracted the bull enough to keep it from hooking Mitch with its horns, but as the animal jumped over Mitch to go after the bullfighters, its back hooves had come down full-force in the middle of Mitch's chest.

With no regard to his own safety, Colt had vaulted the back of the chute and run to protect her brother. After he'd made sure someone was helping Mitch, he had come looking for her in the crush of people behind the chutes. He'd accompanied her to the hospital to wait while Mitch was in surgery. Then later, he'd held her when they received the

news that her only brother—her only living relative—had died on the operating table.

"M-mommy!" a little voice cried from down the
hall.

The sound of her daughter awakening from her
afternoon nap was a welcomed release from the disturbing memories. Setting her coffee cup on the end
table, Kaylee rose from the couch. As she walked
down the hall to see about Amber, Kaylee wiped
away the last of her tears. She had Amber to think
about now. She didn't have time to worry about a
past she couldn't change.

"Did you have a bad dream, sweetie?" she asked,
lifting the little girl from her small bed.

Amber shook her head sleepily, put her finger in
her mouth and buried her face in her mother's neck.

"It's all right. Mommy won't let anything hurt
you," Kaylee said, hugging her daughter close.

She started into the living room to sit in the rocking chair with Amber, but the ringing door bell had
her detouring to see who the current salesman was
and what he was trying to sell today. Turning on the
tape player she kept by the door, she smiled at Amber as the sounds of a snarling German Shepard
filled the room.

"One of these days, Mommy's going to get a real
dog with enormous teeth and an insatiable appetite
for door-to-door salesmen." Making sure the security chain was in place, Kaylee took a deep breath

and reached for the doorknob. "Until then, let's see how fast we can send this joker on his way."

As Colt waited at the door to the second-floor apartment, he adjusted the sling holding his left arm snug against his body and looked around at the shabby building. What was Kaylee doing here instead of living on her ranch up in the Oklahoma panhandle?

While he'd been recuperating last month, he'd done a lot of soul-searching and had come to the realization that he had to find her and make things right. He shook his head. He'd been ready to jump on that paramedic for his lack of respect toward her, yet, to his chagrin, he'd realized that he hadn't acted any better. He'd snapped at her for no other reason than the fact that she'd witnessed him give in to the pain of a broken collarbone like some little kid.

But when he'd gotten back on his feet, he'd gone to the Lazy S only to find that Kaylee had sold the ranch and moved to Oklahoma City shortly after Mitch had died. He'd had to resort to searching through the phone book to find her. Fortunately there'd only been one Kaylee Simpson listed in the area.

The door suddenly opened as far as the security chain would allow. "I don't care what you're selling. I don't want—" Kaylee stopped abruptly. "Colt?"

Pushing the wide brim of his Resistol up with his thumb, he rocked back on his heels, chuckling at the recording of a snarling dog. "Does that tape of Kujo really chase off door-to-door salesmen?"

She stared at him through the narrow opening as if she couldn't quite believe her eyes. "W-what are you doing here?"

He winced at her blunt tone. She sure didn't seem very happy to see him. All things considered, he couldn't say that he blamed her.

Hoping to tease her into a better mood, he grinned. "Well, hello to you, too, brat. You want to shut off Kujo, now that you know it's me and not somebody trying to sell a vacuum cleaner?"

She turned away and the sound of the snarling dog ceased. "I'm sorry. Hello, Colt."

"Me see," a little voice said a moment before a set of tiny fingers appeared around the edge of the door in an effort to open it wider.

Colt frowned. "Do you have company?"

"No, but this really isn't a good time," Kaylee said, prying the baby's fingers from the door.

The panic suddenly filling her violet eyes bothered him. A lot. "Are you all right, Kaylee?"

She nodded. "I'm fine."

"Me see, Mommy," the little voice insisted. "Me see."

"Not now, sweetie," Kaylee said gently.

Colt felt as though he'd been sucker punched. Kaylee had a child? Was she married?

"We need to talk," he said seriously.

He told himself that Mitch would want Colt to make sure she was doing okay. But the truth was, he wanted to know what was going on.

"I can't imagine what you think we need to talk about." She gave him a one-shouldered shrug, but he could tell from the tone of her voice that she was nervous as hell about something.

"Come on, Kaylee," he said, watching her closely. "I drove all the way down here from the Lonetree just to talk to you. The least you can do is give me five minutes."

Her defeated expression caused the air to lodge in his lungs. Something was definitely going on, and Colt had every intention of finding out what is was.

"Kaylee?"

She closed the door, released the chain, then swung it wide for him to step into the tiny apartment. "I'm sorry about the mess," she said, pointing to the toys scattered on the floor in front of the couch. "I wasn't expecting anyone."

Colt turned to tell her he was used to seeing toys scattered all over his two brothers' homes, but the words died somewhere between his vocal cords and opened mouth. The baby riding Kaylee's hip was a little girl with raven curls. Her face was buried shyly against Kaylee's neck, but something about the child caused his scalp to prickle and his pulse to race.

"Is she yours?" he asked cautiously.

Kaylee stared at him for what seemed like an eternity before she slowly nodded. "Yes. This is my daughter, Amber."

At the sound of her name, the baby looked up, but when she saw him staring at her, she stuck one tiny index finger in her mouth and once again hid her face in Kaylee's shoulder.

The glimpse Colt had gotten hadn't been much, but it was enough to see that the little girl's eyes were blue. A vivid blue. His sisters-in-law, Annie and Samantha, called it "Wakefield blue."

His heart pounding against his ribs like a jungle drum, he had a hard time drawing air into his lungs. The child had to be around the same age as his brother Brant's little boy, Zach. From there it didn't take much for Colt to do the math.

Swallowing hard, he asked, "She's mine, isn't she, Kaylee?"

Colt watched her bite her lower lip to keep it from trembling. He knew the answer, but he needed to hear her tell him.

"Kaylee?"

She took a deep breath, then defiantly met his gaze. "Yes, Colt. Amber is your daughter, too."

Two

"**D**ammit, Kaylee, why didn't you tell me?" Colt demanded. Conflicting emotions twisted his gut and he had to force himself to take several deep breaths in an effort to stay calm. "Didn't you think I had the right to know about my own daughter?"

Anger flashed in her violet eyes. "No."

Colt wasn't sure how he'd expected her to answer, but the vehemence in her tone surprised him. He'd never seen her this angry before.

"Why not?" he asked, his own anger flaring.

If anyone had the right to be pissed off here, it was him. Kaylee had been the one who kept him from knowing about his child.

The baby started to whimper and clutch at her mother. Apparently their raised voices were upsetting her.

"Would you like to have some juice, sweetie?" Kaylee asked, her voice once again soft and gentle as she rubbed the little girl's back.

The child nodded.

"Let me get her settled down." Kaylee's voice was calm, but the look she gave him was pure defiance. "Then we'll talk."

"You're damned right we will," he muttered, watching her carry her daughter—his daughter—into the kitchenette.

His daughter.

Colt's chest swelled with a feeling he'd never before experienced. He was the daddy of a two-year-old child—a little girl who looked just like him. The thought caused a lump to form in his throat and made it hard as hell for him to drag air into his lungs.

As the knowledge sank in, questions flooded his mind. How could Kaylee have done this to him? Why hadn't she let him know that their only night together had made her pregnant?

He wasn't sure what her reasons had been, but he had every intention of finding out. Removing his cowboy hat, he set it down beside a tape player on a shelf by the door. He wasn't going anywhere until Kaylee gave him some answers. And, he decided as he ran a frustrated hand through his thick hair, they'd better be damned good ones.

Kaylee brushed past him to set Amber on the floor with her toys. He waited until she handed the toddler a small plastic glass he'd heard his sisters-in-law refer to as a sippy cup before he asked, "Were you ever going to tell me about her?"

Kaylee picked up a mug from the coffee table. "No."

Shocked, Colt started to ask her why, but she stopped him by motioning for him to follow her into the kitchen. Walking behind her, he tried not to notice that her cutoff jeans hugged her cute little rear to perfection, or the fact that they exposed a lot more of her long, slender legs than they covered. When she reached up to get another coffee cup out of the cabinet for him, he swallowed hard. Her hot-pink tank top pulled away from the waistband of her cutoffs and gave him more than a fair view of her smooth, flat abdomen.

He shook his head. What the hell was wrong with him? Kaylee had not only kept his only child a secret from him, she was Mitch's little sister. And although Colt had given in to temptation once, he couldn't—wouldn't—let it happen again.

Pouring them both a cup of coffee, she indicated that he should sit at the small table. When he lowered himself into a chair, she seated herself across from him so that she could watch their daughter play with a small teddy bear.

"As far as I'm concerned, you never needed to know about Amber," she said, glaring at him.

Anger and confusion raced through him and he had to wait a moment before he could speak. Losing his cool wouldn't net him the answers he needed.

"Being pregnant was the reason you took that year off from school, wasn't it?" he asked, suddenly understanding her evasive answers in the training room the night he'd been injured.

"Yes."

"You should have told me," he said, trying to keep his voice even. "I would have helped."

"I didn't want or need your assistance." Her voice shook with emotion. "I never wanted you to know about Amber."

"Why, Kaylee?" He'd never seen her this stubborn. But then, he was just as determined. "What made you think I didn't have the right to know that I'd fathered a child?"

"You gave up the right," she said without looking at him. Her voice was a little more calm, but her words couldn't have held more resolution.

His own irritation won over his vow to remain coolheaded. "How the hell do you figure that?"

"The morning after Mitch's funeral I got the message loud and clear." She met his gaze head-on and the mixture of hurt and resentment sparkling in her eyes stopped him cold. "You wanted nothing more to do with me. When I discovered I was pregnant, I assumed those feelings would encompass my baby, as well."

The guilt that had plagued him for the past three years increased tenfold. He'd not only slept with his best friend's sister the night after they'd laid the man to rest, he'd taken her virginity. Colt knew that he'd handled things badly the morning after he'd made love to her, but he'd been so ashamed of his actions, he hadn't been able to face himself let alone her.

"Kaylee, that's not the way it was. I—"

"Oh, really?" she interrupted hotly. "Just how many times in the past three years have you tried to get in touch with me, Colt?"

He didn't think it was possible to feel lower than he already did, but Kaylee had just proven him wrong. "I know that if they handed out prizes for tactless jackasses, I'd win hands down. But there's a reason—"

"Too little, too late," she said, rising to her feet. "I'm really not interested in hearing why you left that morning without waking me or even leaving a note." She picked up his untouched coffee and poured it down the sink.

"Hey, I'm not finished with—"

"Yes, you are." She walked to the door. "I'd appreciate it if you'd go now. All I'm interested in is you leaving Amber…and me alone. We've done just fine…without you.''

He detected the hitch in Kaylee's voice and knew she was fighting tears. The thought that he'd caused her such emotional pain made him feel physically ill.

Taking a deep breath, he rose and followed her. He needed time to come to grips with everything that he'd learned in the past hour, as well as to figure out how to make Kaylee listen to him.

''I think it would be best if we continue this conversation after we've both had a chance—''

''No, Colt,'' she said, shaking her head. ''You gave up that chance three years ago when you left me behind without a backward glance. You got what you wanted, now let me have…what I want.''

The single tear sliding down her pale cheek just about tore him apart. ''What do you want, Kaylee?''

She took a deep breath and impatiently wiped the droplet away with a trembling hand, then pointed toward the door. ''I want you to walk out…the way you did that morning three years ago and…never look back.''

''I can't do that, honey,'' he said, reaching out to wipe another tear from her satiny skin with the pad of his thumb. ''I'll be back tomorrow after we've both calmed down.''

''Please…don't.'' Tears coursed down her cheeks unchecked as she stepped away from his touch. ''It would be best…if you went back…to the Lonetree Ranch in Wyoming and forgot…we exist.''

''That's not going to happen,'' Colt said gently.

He picked up his Resistol and placed it on his head, then looked over at Amber playing quietly with her toys. She was curiously watching him. But the moment she realized he was looking back at her, she smiled shyly and hid her face behind the teddy bear in her tiny hands.

He fell in love with his daughter right then and there.

''I'll see you tomorrow.'' Turning to open the door, he didn't think twice about leaning down to place a kiss on Kaylee's tear-stained cheek. ''We'll get all of this worked out, honey. I promise.''

The next day Kaylee nervously sat at the kitchen table awaiting Colt's return. She dreaded the upcoming confrontation, but at the same time, a small part of her looked forward to seeing him again. And that was a huge problem.

She'd fallen in love with Colt Wakefield almost the moment she'd met him. Her mother had called it a schoolgirl crush and told her that she'd grow out of it in time. But Kaylee had always known better. Over the years her feelings for him hadn't diminished, they'd only grown stronger.

But after that fateful morning when she'd awakened to find him gone, she'd forced herself to forget about him and to move on. She'd had to. She wouldn't have survived the past few years if she hadn't.

Unfortunately she'd discovered yesterday afternoon that he still affected her in ways she thought she'd put behind her. When Colt touched her, she'd felt the familiar racing of her heart, the jolt of excitement that being near him had always caused. But the most disturbing discovery of all had been the fact that he still had the power to cause her emotional pain.

"Mommy, see!"

Kaylee looked up to watch Amber laugh and point to the animated vegetables dancing and singing their way across the television screen.

Smiling, she walked into the living room to join her daughter. "You like that don't you, sweetie?"

"No," Amber said, her soft shoulder-length curls bouncing as she nodded her little head affirmatively.

Kaylee grinned. One of these days Amber would get the words and the body language synchronized. As she gazed at her daughter, Kaylee was once again struck by how much Amber looked like Colt. The resemblance was amazing, and she had known the minute he saw Amber that he'd realize she was his child. She had the same dark hair and vivid blue eyes that all the Wakefields shared.

Lost in thought, the ringing doorbell caused her to jump and sent Amber scurrying to wrap her arms around Kaylee's legs. Amber wasn't used to strangers and tended to be extremely shy.

Picking her daughter up, Kaylee didn't bother turning on the snarling dog tape as she moved to answer the door. There was no need. She knew who would be waiting on the other side.

"Hi," Colt said when she opened the door. He picked up a shopping bag sitting at his booted feet. "Sorry I'm a little late, but I stopped by a toy store to get something for Amber."

Amber's face was already buried in Kaylee's neck and the sound of Colt's deep baritone saying her name caused her to tighten her little arms around Kaylee's neck.

Stepping away for him to enter, Kaylee patted Amber's back in an effort to soothe her. "I see you didn't bother listening to me yesterday when I asked you to leave us alone."

His smile sent a shiver up her spine. "Did you really expect me to?"

"No." She sighed heavily. Why did he have to be so darned good-looking? So charming?

"Amber, I brought you something," he said softly.

"She's not used to strangers," Kaylee said when Amber continued to keep her face hidden. "And especially men."

Colt's piercing blue eyes met hers and she could tell that he was speculating about her social life—

specifically her social life with men. "She hasn't been around a lot of men?" he finally asked.

"Not really," Kaylee answered evasively.

If circumstances had been different, she might have laughed out loud. She hadn't been out on a date in the past three years. But Colt didn't need to know that.

The cad had the audacity to look relieved. "That's going to change," he said, sounding quite confident. "She'll get used to me being around all the time."

All the time?

Kaylee's heart skipped a beat. She definitely didn't like the sound of that. She'd done a lot of thinking since yesterday afternoon and she'd conceded that she couldn't deny Amber the chance to get to know the man who was responsible for her existence. But there were going to be limits set.

"Colt, I don't think that would be a good idea."

"Why not?" he asked, wincing as he adjusted the sling holding his left arm immobile.

"Do you still have a lot of pain from the broken collarbone?" She hoped to divert the conversation into safer territory.

"Not really." He removed his Resistol and placed it on the shelf with her tape player. "But I anticipate that will change when I start physical therapy."

"If the therapy is done right, and you don't over-work your shoulder too soon, you shouldn't have anything more than a little minor soreness.'' When she felt Amber begin to loosen her hold, signaling that she was becoming accustomed to Colt's presence, Kaylee walked over to sit her daughter down in front of the television. ''When do you start therapy?''

''In another week or two,'' he answered. ''I've been doing some simple range-of-motion stuff, but that's about it.''

She heard him rummage through the shopping bag and, when she turned around, watched him struggle to pull out a large rag doll. Unable to use both of his hands, he'd gotten the doll tangled in the bag handles.

''Let me,'' she said, walking over to help him. Reaching to work the doll's leg free, his hand touched hers. Kaylee jerked back from the scorching contact and handed the doll to him. ''A-Amber will like this.''

He stared at her for several long seconds before he cleared his throat and asked, ''Do you think it would frighten her if I gave it to her now?''

The look on his handsome face took Kaylee by surprise. It was the first time she ever remembered seeing Colt look uncertain.

''Maybe in a few minutes. She's just getting adjusted to you being here.'' Kaylee's heart went out to him even if she wasn't particularly comfortable with the feeling. It was clear Colt wanted to get to know Amber, but didn't want to do anything that would upset her. "Let's sit in the living room. You'll be close to her, but not so much that she'll feel threatened."

"Okay. We can talk while Amber gets used to me." He followed her over to sit on the couch, and she could feel his gaze on her backside just as surely as if he touched her.

When they were settled on the sagging blue cushions, Kaylee found it hard to breathe. Glancing at her daughter to keep from looking at Colt, she noticed Amber looking at them curiously.

"It's all right, sweetie. Colt is a friend."

"I'm your daddy," he said, his voice gentle. Turning to Kaylee, he firmly added, "I don't want her to ever doubt that."

Amber didn't seem to pick up on the sudden tension between the two adults as she turned her attention back to the television.

But Kaylee did, and it only served to increase her apprehension. Hoping to take the lead in what she knew would be a difficult conversation, she said, "Colt, I've done a lot of thinking about our situation—"

"I haven't been able to think of anything else," he said, nodding. "And this isn't something that can be resolved overnight."

"No, it's not. It's going to take time for us—"

"I'm glad you agree," he said, smiling. "It will make everything a lot easier on all concerned."

Where was he going with this? And why did he keep interrupting her?

"What's going on, Colt?" she asked, not at all sure she wanted to know.

"I doubt that you're going to like what I'm going to suggest."

She doubted that she would, either. His tone was relaxed, but from the serious look on his face, she could tell he was anything but nonchalant about what he was going to say.

"Tell me what you have in mind and we'll see," she said cautiously.

"I want you and Amber to come back to the Lonetree with me."

She couldn't believe he'd come up with something so outlandish. "You can't be serious."

"I'm very serious, Kaylee." The determination in his brilliant blue eyes startled her. "I intend to get to know my daughter."

"You can get to know Amber right here," she argued. There was no way she would agree to go to his ranch in Wyoming.

"No, I can't." He turned his gaze to watch Amber play quietly with some of her toys. "If I tried to get to know her here, I'd just end up being some guy who stopped by once in a while and who she'd end up forgetting between visits."

"It works for other fathers," Kaylee insisted, feeling desperate. She had to make him see reason. "It would work for you and Amber."

Colt shook his head. "Maybe if I'd been part of her life from the beginning, but not now." He glanced back at Amber. "I'm going to be her daddy, not just a man who claims to be her father."

Kaylee shook her head. "I can't take time off at the hospital. I'd lose my job."

"No, you won't." His knowing grin sent a chill slithering up her spine. "I've already talked to your superior."

"You did what?" Her temper flared and she had to concentrate hard on keeping her voice even so as not to upset Amber. "You couldn't possibly have talked to anyone about my taking time off. It's Sunday. The physical therapy unit is closed."

"I have my ways," he said, sounding so darned smug that she was sorely tempted to belt him one.

But thinking about what he said, Kaylee suddenly felt cold all over. "What did you do?"

He casually rested his right arm along the back of the couch. "I got in touch with Dr. Carson and had him find out which hospital sent you over to work the PBR event last month. He also gave me the name and phone number of your boss."

Kaylee couldn't believe Colt's arrogance. "You called Brad at home?"

Grinning, Colt nodded. "Once I explained the situation—"

She felt the blood drain from her face. She'd made it a point not to discuss anything about her private life with her co-workers. "Please, tell me you didn't—"

He shook his head as he played with a lock of her hair. "No, honey, I didn't tell him the whole story. That's nobody's business but ours. But I did tell him there was a family crisis that needed your attention and asked if you could get a couple of months off." He smiled. "All you'll have to do is stop by the office tomorrow to sign the papers for your leave of absence."

Anger so intense that she actually started shaking ran through her. "How dare you?" Unable to sit still, Kaylee rose to pace the length of the small living room. "It's one thing for you to walk in and start telling me you want to be a part of my daughter's life, but—"

"Our daughter," he corrected.

Upset by the angry voices, Amber started to cry. She crawled over to Kaylee and wrapped her arms around her mother's leg. "M-mommy!"

Ignoring Colt, Kaylee picked up the baby and held her close as she continued. "You can't take matters into your own hands and make a decision like that for me." She stopped to glare at him. "I can't afford to take time off. I have rent, a car payment and—''

"I'll take care of it.''

"Oh, no, you won't.'' She clutched Amber. "I don't want anything from you.''

Standing, he walked over to her. "Be reasonable, Kaylee. The way I see it, I owe you a little over two years of back child support, and besides, I'd like to hire you to help me get back in shape for the PBR finals the first part of November. You can return here after we get back from Vegas.''

"I don't want your money,'' she said stubbornly. "And I won't help you regain your strength just so you can go back into an arena and risk your life riding a bull for eight seconds' worth of thrills.''

"When I come to pick up you and Amber tomorrow morning, I'll stop by the manager's office and take care of the rent, as well as having him see that the utilities are shut off,'' Colt went on as if he hadn't listened to a word she'd said. "Besides, Kaylee, you owe me.''

"Oh, really? How do you figure that?'' she asked hotly.

His intense blue gaze held hers captive. "You deprived me of Amber's first two years. You owe me the right to get to know her now.''

Kaylee felt her life spinning out of control with no way to stop it. She had a frightened baby screaming in her ear and an infuriating, sexy-as-sin cowboy standing over her, telling her that he was taking over her life. It was enough to wear the Rock of Gibraltar down to an insignificant pebble.

"Please, don't do this to me, Colt," she whispered, feeling more trapped than she'd ever felt in her entire life.

He reached out to cup her cheek. "I love Amber, and I want her to love me. Please give us the chance to develop a relationship, Kaylee."

The weight of guilt settling over Kaylee's shoulders couldn't possibly have felt heavier. As much as she disliked having to admit it, she had been unfair to both Colt and Amber by keeping her secret. Kaylee knew beyond a shadow of doubt that no matter how much he wanted to forget their night together had ever happened, he would have loved and cared for his child from the very moment he learned of her existence.

Tears filled Kaylee's eyes. She'd kept Colt from knowing about his child because of her own hurt feelings and disillusion. In the process, she'd deprived Amber of a daddy who cared deeply for her.

"What do you say, Kaylee?" he asked, wiping a tear from her cheek with his thumb. "Will you and Amber came home with me to the Lonetree?"

She gazed up at the man she'd once loved with all her heart and soul. He was right. She did owe him and Amber the time together. But it was going to take everything she had in her to keep her wits about her while she was with him. If she didn't, she wasn't sure she wouldn't end up falling under his magnetic spell all over again. And that was something she couldn't allow herself to do. Her survival depended on it.

"I can't believe I'm actually going to say this," she finally said, feeling her insides shake like a bowl full of Jell-O.

"You'll go?" he asked hopefully.

Taking a deep breath, Kaylee felt as if she was stepping out onto a tight rope with no safety net below. "Yes, we'll go to the Lonetree with you. But only until you get ready to leave for the season finals. Amber and I won't be going to Las Vegas with you."

"We'll see about that."

The smile he sent her way curled her toes and already had her regretting her decision to go to the Lonetree Ranch with him for the next two months.

Three

"**D**ammit all," Colt muttered, cursing the fact that he still couldn't use his left arm. Not being able to use both hands made installing Amber's car seat in his truck extremely difficult.

"Problems?" Kaylee asked.

Turning, he watched her walk toward him. She held Amber in her arms.

"I could use another hand getting this car seat secured," he said, hating that he looked helpless and inadequate in front of her.

Kaylee set Amber on her feet. "Stay right here, sweetie, while Mommy helps Colt with your seat."

"Daddy," he said firmly. "I'm her daddy, Kaylee."

She stared up at him a moment before she gave a quick nod. "I'm going to help your...daddy, Amber."

Her reluctance to acknowledge him as Amber's father cut like a knife, but Colt ignored it. Once they got to the Lonetree they'd have plenty of time to sort things out and, hopefully, to rebuild the friendship they'd once shared. It would make their raising Amber together a whole hell of a lot easier.

A small sound caught Colt's attention. Glancing down, he noticed his daughter curiously watching him. But the moment she saw him look at her, she ducked behind Kaylee's leg.

"How long do you think it will take for her to be comfortable with me?" he asked, wondering the same thing about Kaylee. Would she ever again be at ease when she was around him?

"I'm not sure." She stared at him for endless seconds before she added, "This is new territory for all of us. It's going to take time."

Colt knew she was referring more to herself than their daughter. Deciding not to push for more, he reached into the truck to position the car seat. "Are you about ready to leave? I'd like to get on the road. We have a long drive and I'd like to get as far as we can before we stop for the night."

"Stop?"

When she turned to look at him, Kaylee's breast brushed his arm. His mouth went as dry as a pile of sawdust. ''I—'' he had to stop to clear his throat ''—thought it would probably be best for Amber if we broke the trip into two days.''

It took everything Colt had in him not to groan out loud when Kaylee's tongue darted out to moisten her perfect coral lips. ''You're probably right,'' she finally answered. Backing away from him, she picked up Amber and started toward the stairs leading to the second floor of the apartment building. ''I'll go check to make sure we brought all of the luggage down and grab Amber's bag of toys.''

Colt waited until Kaylee climbed the steps and disappeared into her apartment before he finally managed to take another breath. Glancing at his scuffed boots, he kicked a pebble and watched it skitter across the asphalt parking lot. He hated that he'd had to resort to making her feel guilty to get her to go to the Lonetree with him. But, dammit, he needed time to get to know Amber, time to work out some kind of shared custody agreement, and time to make amends with Kaylee for what had happened three years ago.

He ran his hand around the back of his neck in an effort to ease some of the tension that had knotted his muscles since Saturday afternoon and his discovery that he'd fathered a child. How was he ever going to convince Kaylee that she wasn't the reason he'd walked away that morning? How was he going to explain that he'd felt as if he'd betrayed Mitch's friendship? And how was he going to make her understand that he'd been so ashamed of his actions, he hadn't been able to face himself, let alone face her?

"If they gave medals for screwing up, you'd win hands down, Wakefield," he muttered disgustedly.

He wasn't quite sure how to go about doing it, but he was determined to straighten everything out with Kaylee. He had to. His, hers and Amber's future happiness depended on it.

"Out, Mommy, out," Amber said, impatiently tugging on the harness holding her in the car seat.

"Just a few more minutes, sweetie," Kaylee answered as she watched Colt enter the motel lobby. "Colt…your daddy is going to get a couple of rooms for us to sleep in tonight."

Amber blinked and nodded her head. "Not seepy."

"I know you're not sleepy right now," Kaylee said, smiling. "But you will be later."

She absently watched Colt as he talked to the desk clerk. He'd decided to stop in Hays, Kansas, for the night even though it was early and they could have driven for several more hours. His excuse had been that he didn't want the trip to be too tiring for Amber. But Kaylee suspected his collarbone bothered him. She also knew that if that was the case, he'd never admit it. For Colt and most of the other cowboys on the PBR and professional rodeo circuits, admitting any kind of weakness was unheard of.

"Did you get rooms on the ground floor or the second level?" Kaylee asked when he got back into the truck.

"Ground floor." He put the truck into gear. "I figured it would be easier."

She didn't have to ask what he meant. She already knew. He intended to carry what few bags they took to their rooms himself, just as he'd insisted on carrying all of her luggage from the apartment to his truck this morning. Unable to use his left arm, it had taken him several trips to get everything downstairs, but he wouldn't hear of her helping.

"I'll carry our bag to mine and Amber's room," she said firmly when he pulled into a parking space at the side of the stucco building.

"Our room."

Kaylee stopped unbuckling Amber's shoulder harness to stare at him. "You rented only one room?"

"Yep."

Her heart hammered against her rib cage. "There weren't any more available?"

"I don't know how many they had available," he answered, sounding so darned unconcerned she wanted to throttle him. "I didn't ask."

When he moved to get out of the truck, she took

hold of his arm to stop him. "You want to give me a reason for not getting the second room?" she asked, doing her best to keep her voice level.

The feel of Colt's rock-hard muscles beneath his red shirt sent a tingle arrowing up her arm. She immediately let go of his bicep to rub her palm on her jeans-clad thigh.

For the first time since getting back into the truck, Colt looked uncertain. "I don't like having to admit this, but I'm probably going to need your help tonight and in the morning."

"With your sling?" Kaylee asked, surprised that he'd admit needing assistance with anything. Because of her training she knew he probably did have trouble trying to put the restraint on with one hand, but she could help him without them spending the night in the same room.

He nodded. "I have a hard time getting it adjusted." He looked thoroughly disgusted. "Trying to get it comfortable is a pain in the—"

Kaylee loudly cleared her throat and nodded toward Amber. "She picks up certain words faster than others."

His charming grin sent a shiver straight up her spine. "I was going to say, it's a pain in the butt."

"I just assumed—"

"The worst," he finished for her as he opened the truck door. When he walked around to open the passenger door, he smiled. "Since Morgan's and

Brant's kids came along, we've all learned to watch what we say.''

"How are your brothers?" she asked, turning to lift Amber from her car seat.

Colt grinned. "Ornery as ever."

Kaylee smiled. She'd always liked Colt's older brothers. "How many children do they have now?"

"Morgan and his wife, Samantha, have two boys," he said, placing his palm to her back to steer her toward their room. "Brant and Annie have one son and, if the sonogram is correct, another one on the way."

"H-heaven help us. Another generation of Wakefield boys," Kaylee said, feeling as if she'd been branded by his warm touch. She quickly put distance between them.

"Yes, but now there's a Wakefield girl," he said, gazing down at Amber as he fit the key card into the lock.

Kaylee swallowed hard at the look of genuine affection on his handsome face. No matter what he felt for her, she knew for certain that he'd fallen head over heels in love with their daughter.

Feeling guilty for keeping Amber from him, she quickly stepped into the motel room and looked around to distract herself. She was relieved to see there were two beds.

"Which bag did you want me to bring in?" Colt asked from behind her.

She set Amber down. "I'll get it."

"No, you won't." He'd already turned to go back outside to the truck.

"Don't be ridiculous, Colt," she said, following him. "With your arm in a sling you'll have to make two trips. I'm perfectly capable of carrying one small overnight bag. It just makes more sense—"

When he spun around to face her, her breath caught at his deep scowl. "I may need help getting this da—dumb sling adjusted, but I'm not helpless. I'll carry the luggage. Now, which one do you want?"

She blew out a frustrated breath. "The red one."

"Wed one," Amber repeated from behind Kaylee's leg.

Colt's expression softened instantly. "Was she actually talking to me?"

"Maybe." He looked so hopeful, Kaylee didn't have the heart to tell him that, like most two-year-old children, Amber parroted a lot of what she heard.

Bending, he asked, "Do you want Daddy to get the red one, Amber?"

Amber smiled up at him a moment before she clutched Kaylee's leg and hid her face.

"Did you see that?" he asked incredulously. He straightened to his full six-foot height. "She actually looked at me for a second or two before she dived for cover."

Kaylee could tell from his expression that the small gesture meant the world to him. "I'd say you're making progress."

"It's a start," he agreed, opening the door to go out to the truck for their overnight bags.

When he closed the door behind him, Kaylee scooped Amber up into her arms. "Colt may be new to this father business, but I think he's going to be a good daddy, don't you, sweetie?"

To Kaylee's astonishment, Amber stared at her for a moment then, pointing to the door, nodded as if in complete agreement.

Sweat beaded Colt's forehead and upper lip as he braced himself on the motel-room desk with his right hand, bent slightly forward and let his left arm dangle in front of him. Taking a deep breath, he gritted his teeth and started another set of range-of-motion exercises. He was supposed to stop after the third set, but he figured if three were good, five had to be better.

"Colt, how many sets of those have you already completed?" Kaylee asked, walking out of the bathroom with Amber.

"Four," he answered without looking up.

He'd wanted to be done with the exercises before she finished giving Amber a bath. Apparently he'd miscalculated the time it would take for the extra sets.

Kaylee's eyes narrowed. "You weren't supposed to do more than three sets, were you?"

"Nope. But three sets, twice a day just isn't enough," he said through gritted teeth. He took a deep breath. He hadn't anticipated the extra exercises taking this much out of him.

"Stop right now!"

At the sharp rise of her voice, he stopped to look up at her. "What?"

"By doing more than is recommended, you could do more damage," she said, sitting Amber in the middle of the bed. Turning back to face him, she propped her hands on her shapely hips as she glared at him. "You're just as stubborn as you always were. Are you even supposed to be in a sling yet, or should you still be wearing a Figure 8 splint?"

"I hated that splint." Careful to keep his shoulder in the same position, he slowly straightened. "I wore that dam—danged thing for about two weeks before I threw it away. I couldn't manage it by myself and I was tired of asking for Morgan and Brant's help."

"So you just took it upon yourself to graduate to a sling, instead of waiting for an orthopedist to say you're ready?" She gave him a look that clearly said she thought he was a few bricks shy of a full load. "Have you been using the sling day and night, or have you been trying to go without it, too?"

He bent his left elbow and held his arm close to

his body while he tried to unsnap his shirt with his right hand. "Unless I'm taking a shower, I wear it all the time."

She stepped forward to help him with the snaps on his Western-style shirt. "Have you experienced any excess pain since you stopped wearing the splint?"

"No, and I'm not having a whole lot of discomfort now." *At least, not the painful kind,* he added silently.

"Only because I stopped you," she said sternly.

He felt his body spring to life as her delicate fingers worked each one of the grippers open. "Would you mind telling me what you think you're doing, Kaylee?"

"I'm helping you take your shirt off for your shower." When she reached the snap just above his belt buckle, she stopped to tug the tail of the garment from the waistband of his jeans.

Her hand brushed his stomach and it felt as if a charge of electricity ran straight through him. It took everything he had in him not to groan out loud.

"I can do this myself," he said through clenched teeth.

"Oh, really?" She stopped to give him a withering glare. "Wasn't it your idea to get *one* room because you needed my assistance?"

"Well, yes, but—"

"Then stop arguing and let me help you."

Unsnapping his right cuff, she reached up to slide the sleeve off his shoulder. Her soft hands on his skin sent heat streaking through his veins and he found it hard to pull air into his lungs.

"I meant..." He had to stop to clear his suddenly dry throat. "—I'd need help with the sling."

She ignored his protest and started to unfasten the cuff at his left wrist. "And I suppose it's easy to get your shirt off and on by yourself."

Her fingertips feathered over his pulse and he had to concentrate hard on what she'd said. "I didn't say...it was easy."

"Could you please tell me something?" she asked, easing his shirt off his left shoulder and down his arm.

The room suddenly seemed warmer with his shirt off than it had with the garment on. "What's... that?"

"Tell me why men can't accept help when they need it, or ask for directions when they have no idea where they're going," she said, draping his shirt over the desk chair.

"We don't—" He stopped abruptly when she brought her hands to his waist and started to work his belt through the metal buckle. "W-what are you...doing, Kaylee?"

"You said you'd need my help," she said, pulling the leather strap from the belt loops of his jeans. "And that's...just what you're going to get."

She sounded angry, but the hitch in her voice suggested she was as affected by helping him out of his clothes as he was by having her take them off him.

"Kaylee—"

He wasn't sure what he was about to say, but he stopped short at the sound of Amber's giggles. Turning his attention to his daughter, Colt didn't think he'd ever seen anything as precious as her happy expression.

"You think seeing your mommy yell at Daddy is funny?" he asked, grinning.

Giggling delightedly, the baby grabbed the doll he'd bought her and hid behind it.

Distracted by Amber's laughter, it took a moment for him to realize that Kaylee was working the metal button free at his waistband. Heat shot through his veins and made a beeline straight to his groin.

"I think…" His voice cracked like a kid going through puberty. "…I can handle it from here."

She gave him another one of those looks that a woman gives a man when she thinks he's being a stubborn fool. "Oh, for heaven's sake, I'm a trained medical professional and I've assisted dozens of people with their clothes." She reached for the tab of his zipper. "Besides, we both know you're no more attracted to me than I am to you, so it's not an issue."

From the heightened color on her cheeks and the hesitation in her voice, he knew her statement that

she wasn't attracted to him was an outright lie. But
at the moment, that wasn't an immediate concern. If
he didn't stop her—and damn quick—it wouldn't
take more than another second or two and she'd see
the evidence of just how alluring he found her.

Grabbing her hand, Colt shook his head. "I said
I'd take care of it."

"Fine." She pointed to the chair. "Have a seat
and I'll take off your boots."

"I can—"

She arched one perfect eyebrow. "How long does
it take you to get them on and off by yourself?"

"I manage," he said defensively. He hated to admit that he struggled more with his boots than anything else.

"Sit down and raise your foot."

Amused by her authoritative tone, he did as she
said and lowered himself onto the chair. But his en-
joyment quickly faded and his mouth went bone-dry
when she turned, straddled his leg and began tugging on his boot. As she worked to remove it, her
cute little rear bobbed in front of his face and sent
his blood pressure into stroke range.

He closed his eyes and tried to think of something—anything—to get his mind off of how close
Kaylee was and how much he'd like to prove her
theory wrong that he didn't find her attractive. But
by the time she'd removed both of his boots, Colt
felt as if he had enough adrenaline pumping through

his veins to bench-press a bulldozer and he was hard-pressed to suck air into his lungs.

"Do you want help with anything else?" she asked, turning to face him.

"No."

He wanted help all right, but it wasn't the kind of aid she was offering. Rising to his feet, he quickly turned to get a change of clothes from his duffel bag before she saw the evidence of the assistance he needed.

"After your shower I'll put the sling back on," she said as she picked up Amber. "Tell your daddy good-night, sweetie."

Grinning, Amber shook her head, hugged Kaylee around the neck and buried her little face in her mother's shoulder.

"At least, she's smiling at me a little more," Colt said, wishing Amber would allow him to hold her.

"More progress," Kaylee said, sounding a little less angry.

Nodding, Colt turned to walk into the bathroom. Slowly but surely, he was winning over his daughter. Now if he could just regain the friendship he once shared with her mother, maybe they could work things out where everyone would be happy.

Long after Kaylee and Amber had fallen asleep, Colt lay in bed thinking about what Kaylee had said while helping him with his clothes. She didn't think he found her attractive.

He turned his head on the pillow to look over at the woman and child sleeping peacefully in the bed next to his. The light they'd left on in the bathroom illuminated the room enough for him to make out their delicate features in the semidarkness.

The idea that any man with a pulse wouldn't be drawn to Kaylee like a bee to honey was so damn ludicrous it was almost laughable. She was intelligent, witty, and so damn sexy that every time he was around her, he found himself fighting a constant state of arousal. Hell, he could even remember the exact moment four years ago when he'd realized that Mitch's younger sister had grown from a skinny, bratty little kid into a beautiful, desirable woman.

It had been a couple of weeks before her twentieth birthday and she'd met him and Mitch at the PBR event in St. Louis, just as she'd always done. But when she'd breezed into the hotel where they'd been staying, Colt had taken one look and it was as if he'd seen her for the first time. He'd suddenly found himself noticing how her silky auburn hair framed her heart-shaped face, how her violet eyes sparkled with life, and how she seemed to light up a room with her smile.

He'd never allowed himself to act on his attraction to her, though. He hadn't dared. If things hadn't worked out between him and Kaylee, Colt might have lost the best friend he'd ever had. And that was something he hadn't been willing to risk.

But everything was different now. Mitch was gone—taken from this world way before his time. And, because of Colt's one night of weakness, he and Kaylee had a child together.

He closed his eyes against the guilt he still felt over the night Amber had been conceived. Due to the devastating blow they'd both suffered from losing Mitch, they'd turned to each other for emotional support. He'd been old enough to know better, and should have called a halt to it, but having Kaylee in his arms had been more temptation than he'd been able to resist. Like a damned fool, he'd allowed comfort to turn to passion and they'd ended up making love.

Colt sighed heavily. She had every right to despise him for taking her virginity and leaving her alone with a baby to care for. God only knew he hated himself enough for what he'd done. But he didn't think Kaylee felt that way. She might try to deny it, but he could tell the chemistry between them was just as strong, if not stronger, than it had ever been.

Unfortunately he wasn't sure that exploring it now, or in the future, would ever be an option for them. They had Amber to consider. And her welfare came first.

His gaze straying to his child, Colt's chest tightened. She looked like a cute little pixie curled up next to Kaylee, and although he'd only known about his daughter a few days, he loved her more than life itself.

Looking back at Kaylee, a deep sense of loss twisted his gut. If they tried for more than friendship and failed, it would only complicate an already complex situation and make raising Amber together extremely difficult.

He took a deep breath and tried to will himself to forget the idea completely. It just wasn't a risk he could afford to take.

But as he drifted off to sleep, Colt dreamed of holding Kaylee's delectable body to his, of having her call his name as he brought her to the brink of ecstasy, and of a future with her that he knew he could never have.

Four

"Colt, is this another way to get to the Lonetree?" Kaylee asked, looking around. She'd been to the ranch several times with Mitch before he died, but they'd never used the road Colt was driving down now.

Steering the truck around a tight curve, he grinned. "Honey, we've been on Lonetree land for the past fifteen minutes."

"I keep forgetting how big this place is," she said, not at all surprised by his answer.

Her family's ranch had been a nice size, but the Lonetree was one of the largest privately owned ranches left in the United States. Most of the other ranches of comparable acreage had been sold off to corporations or divided up into smaller tracts as one generation inherited the land from another. But the Wakefield brothers had decided after their father passed on to keep the Lonetree Ranch intact and to work it together.

"In case you're wondering why we aren't headed north to the homestead, it's because I don't live there anymore," he said matter-of-factly.

Kaylee swallowed hard. She'd been counting on Morgan and his wife to provide a buffer between her and Colt. "If you don't live there, just where *do* you live?"

"Two and a half years ago I decided to build my own place three miles northwest of the homestead," he said, smiling.

She narrowed her eyes as anger swept through her. "You purposely left that little detail out when you asked me to come here."

His easy expression faded. "I didn't think you'd agree if you'd known we wouldn't be staying with Morgan and Samantha."

"You're right." Blowing out a frustrated breath, she folded her arms beneath her breasts. "That's fine. You can take Amber and me to the bus station tomorrow and we'll go back to Oklahoma."

Colt's mouth flattened into a tight line, but he remained silent until they topped a rise overlooking a peaceful-looking valley. "That's my place down there," he said, pointing to the far end of the basin.

Kaylee's breath caught at the sight of a gorgeous two-story log home with a split-rail fence surrounding the yard. Several horses grazed contentedly in the pastures surrounding the structure and a beautiful black stallion pranced in the corral at the side of the big barn.

"Do you like it?" he asked.

"The word 'like' doesn't even begin to describe it," she said as she tried to swallow around the huge lump clogging her throat. Until Mitch's death, she'd lived on a ranch all of her life, and she missed the quiet solitude of an uncluttered landscape. "This is absolutely beautiful, Colt."

"Thanks." He seemed pleased that she liked his home as he steered the truck off the road and onto a narrow gravel lane leading up to the house. "I still have a storage shed I'd like to build next spring, and eventually I'd like to add an indoor arena with a couple of bucking chutes."

At the mention of his wanting to construct an area where he could practice riding bulls, a chill raced through her. She'd lost her enthusiasm for bull riding when she lost her brother to the sport.

Parking the truck beside the house, Colt grinned. "Welcome to my part of the Lonetree, ladies."

Amber giggled and hid her face behind her hands.

"You like Daddy's house?" Colt asked.

Shaking her head, she kept her face hidden but continued to laugh.

Colt's grin widened. ''More progress.''

Kaylee's chest tightened at the love she saw in Colt's expression when he gazed at Amber. No matter what had taken place between her and Colt, Kaylee knew for certain that Amber had a daddy who loved her with all his heart.

She sighed wistfully. There had been a time when she'd dreamed of coming home to the Lonetree with Colt and their child. Only, in her fantasy, they'd been married and hopelessly in love.

She almost laughed at her own foolishness. That had been several years ago—before she'd grown up to realize that the world wasn't made of fairy tales and not every story had a happy ending.

''Kaylee? Are you all right?''

Looking up, she saw that Colt had gotten out of the truck and was standing with the passenger door open. ''I'm fine.'' She unbuckled Amber's shoulder harness, then lifted her daughter from the car seat. ''I was just thinking about how many things have changed over the years.''

He stared at her for a moment before he offered his hand to help her from the truck. He smiled sadly, and she knew he was thinking about Mitch. ''Some things do change, honey. We don't always like it, but we can't stop it.'' When he met her gaze, the look in his vivid blue eyes took her breath. ''But some things stay the same, even if it doesn't seem that they have.''

She had no idea what he meant by his last comment, but deciding it was time to lighten the mood, she set Amber on her feet, then took hold of her hand. ''Does the inside of your house look as good as the outside, or did you decorate in modern bachelor?''

Colt laughed as he guided her up the front porch steps. ''It's actually a combination of modern bachelor and cast-off Wakefield.''

Kaylee grinned. ''Let me guess. You raided the attic at the homestead.''

''Yep.'' Opening the front door, he stepped back for her and Amber to precede him into the house. ''I do have a new recliner and a kick-butt entertainment system, though.''

''That would be the modern bachelor part of the decor, right?'' she asked, leading Amber into the foyer. Before he could answer she caught her breath at her first glimpse of the great room. ''Colt, it's absolutely perfect.''

The golden hue of the log walls and wood floor were perfectly accented by the bright red, blue and yellow Native American print upholstery on the overstuffed couch and matching chairs. Grouped on a huge braided rug in front of the stone fireplace, it made the room very warm and inviting.

''I love the colors and the Western accents,'' she

said, noticing several pieces of vintage leather tack and Native American artifacts hanging on the walls, along with a pair of spurs and a bronze sculpture of a bull and rider on the mantel.

"Samantha and Annie really got into helping me decorate it," he said, sounding pleased. "Annie bought a do-it-yourself book on reupholstering, then coerced Brant and Morgan into helping her with some furniture she and Samantha found in the attic at the homestead. While they recovered the couch and chairs, Samantha made drapes. I came home after a PBR event in Colorado Springs and didn't recognize the place."

"They did a wonderful job," Kaylee said, meaning it. She looked around. "But I thought you said you had a lounger and an entertainment system."

"They're in the family room just off the kitchen," he said, pointing toward one end of the great room. "And there's a weight room back there, too."

Kaylee glanced in the direction he indicated and felt compelled to take a closer look. She wasn't interested in the other rooms as much as she was the kitchen. She loved to cook and had always felt that it was the heart of any home.

Holding Amber's hand so she wouldn't wander off, Kaylee walked past the snack bar separating the two rooms and immediately fell in love with the light oak cabinets, highly polished black-marble countertops and terra-cotta-tiled floor. Everything about the room appealed to her.

"Like it?" Colt asked, leaning one hip against the end of the snack bar.

"What woman wouldn't like it?" she asked, smiling.

A sudden thought caused her smile to fade and a deep sadness to fill her soul. One day Colt would be sharing this beautiful home with a woman, and it wouldn't be her.

"Up, Mommy, up," Amber said, rubbing her eyes with one little fist.

Thankful that she'd been distracted from the disturbing thought, Kaylee picked up her daughter. "It's about time for your nap, isn't it, sweetie?"

Amber shook her head, then laid her cheek on Kaylee's shoulder.

"I don't think she likes admitting that she's sleepy," Colt said, smiling.

Kaylee nodded. "She's afraid she'll miss something." She glanced toward the family room. "Is there somewhere I could lay her down once she goes to sleep?"

"I guess the couch in the family room would be best," he said, looking thoughtful. "I think the first order of business will be to borrow a crib from Morgan or Brant, and a couple of those gates they put up to keep their kids away from the stairs."

When Kaylee nodded her agreement, then carried

Amber into the family room, Colt released a relieved breath. He couldn't believe how good it felt to know Kaylee liked his home. He really hadn't expected her opinion to mean so much to him.

But at the moment he had a more pressing concern than Kaylee's approval. He hadn't been prepared for a toddler, and the house needed to be child-proofed for Amber's safety.

He took a deep breath, then crossed the great room to enter the study. He wasn't looking forward to the phone call he was about to make. No matter which brother he called to borrow the items needed to make the house safe, he was going to get the third degree.

Deciding Brant was the less intense of his two brothers, Colt picked up the phone and punched in the number. "Hey, bro," he said when Brant answered. "I need a favor."

Twenty minutes later, when Colt parked the truck in his brother's driveway, he wasn't at all surprised to see Brant standing on the porch waiting for him.

"Okay, little brother, spill it," Brant said as soon as Colt opened the driver's door. "Why do you need all of this baby stuff?"

"Hello to you, too, bro," Colt said, stalling.

He'd told his brother he would explain everything when he arrived to pick up the portable crib and other items he'd requested. But he sure as hell wasn't looking forward to it.

Both of his brothers liked Kaylee a lot. They'd known her almost as long as Colt had, and from the time they'd figured out that she had a huge crush on him, they'd warned him not to hurt her, unless he wanted to answer to both of them. Now, meeting his grim-faced brother's stormy gaze, Colt knew for certain Brant wasn't going to like what he was about to hear any more than Colt liked having to tell him.

Deciding there was no better way to break the news than straight-out, Colt took a deep breath. "I need the crib for my daughter, Amber."

Clearly dumbfounded, it took a moment for Brant to respond. "Let me get this straight. You have a daughter named Amber, and she's staying with you?"

"Yep."

"Her mom is with her?" Brant asked, his frown darkening.

"She's getting Amber down for a nap," Colt said, nodding. "That's why I need to get the stuff and get back."

Brant shook his head. "You're not getting off that easy, little brother. You left out a whole bunch of real important details. Like, how old Amber is, how long you've known about her and her mother's name."

Pushing his Resistol back with his thumb, Colt

sighed heavily and sat on the porch steps. "You might want to have a seat."

"I don't like the sound of this," Brant said, sitting beside him.

"Well, I'm none to wild about having to tell you about it, either," Colt said, staring out across the pasture. He should have known Brant wasn't going to settle for a bare-bones account of what was going on. "Amber is a couple of months younger than Zach," he finally said, referring to Brant's little boy. "And I didn't know anything about her until four days ago."

Brant whistled low. "That's unfair," he said, his voice filled with understanding. "I'm sorry to hear the woman didn't see fit to let you know. Do I know her?"

"Yeah." Colt glanced at his brother from the corner of his eye. "Kaylee is Amber's mother."

From his stunned expression, Brant looked as though he'd been treated to the business end of a cattle prod. "Kaylee Simpson?"

Nodding, Colt didn't say anything as he waited for his brother to digest the news. It didn't take long.

"What the hell were you thinking?" Brant demanded, his dark scowl formidable. "Besides the fact that Morgan and I both warned you not to hurt Kaylee, why didn't you make sure you protected her?"

Colt rubbed at the tension gripping the muscles

at the back of his neck, then readjusted his sling to a more comfortable position. "Neither one of us was doing a whole lot of thinking that night. We were both too torn up over losing Mitch." He took a deep breath and met his brother's gaze head-on. "I swear I didn't intend to sleep with Kaylee that night. But as soon as I saw my little girl, I knew I wasn't sorry that I had."

Brant's deep frown faded as his eyes filled with understanding. "I felt the same way the first time I looked at Zach. But that doesn't explain why Kaylee didn't tell you when she found out she was pregnant."

Staring out across the pasture, Colt shrugged his good shoulder. He wasn't proud of his actions, nor was he eager to share the details. "Let's just say she had her reasons, and leave it at that."

Brant nodded. "I guess that explains why none of us has seen or heard from Kaylee since Mitch died."

"Yeah." Colt sighed heavily. "It also explains why she turned down Morgan's request last year when he e-mailed to see if she'd teach horseback riding at Samantha's camp for underprivileged kids."

"How *did* you find out about Amber?" Brant asked suddenly.

"I stopped by Kaylee's place to see how she's been. When she opened the door, she was holding

Amber.'' Colt met Brant's questioning gaze. ''All it took was one look and I knew Amber was my little girl.''

''She looks like a Wakefield?''

''Same black hair and blue eyes,'' Colt said, nodding.

They sat in silence for some time before Brant asked, ''Are you going to marry Kaylee?''

Colt whipped his head around to stare at his brother. ''Did you work the PBR event this past weekend?'' One of the best rodeo bullfighters in the country, Brant worked most of the PBR events plus several of the major professional rodeos.

Brant looked puzzled. ''Yeah, but what does that have to do with—''

''You must have taken a pretty good hit and ended up landing on your head,'' Colt said disgustedly. ''How do you figure Kaylee would want to marry me if she wouldn't even tell me she was pregnant?''

''Have you asked her?''

''No.''

''Then how do you know she wouldn't?'' Brant asked seriously.

''I just know,'' Colt said, shaking his head.

He'd already thought about asking Kaylee to be his wife when he first found out about Amber. But it had taken him all of about two seconds to come to his senses. Even if Kaylee was willing to marry him, which he knew for certain she wasn't, they had Amber's happiness to think of. Getting married for the wrong reasons could prove disastrous.

What would happen if their marriage didn't work? Amber could be hurt worse by a breakup than if they never married at all.

"But you are going to make things right between the two of you?" Brant asked.

Colt nodded. "That's why I brought Kaylee and Amber home with me. First and foremost, I'm going to do some major fence-mending."

"Good idea," Brant said. "I don't know what happened between you, but I do know Kaylee. Whatever it was had to be pretty bad for her not to tell you about your daughter."

"It wasn't one of my prouder moments," Colt admitted, his gut twisting when he thought about how badly he'd handled the situation. "But after I make amends for being a real bonehead, I want to see if we can't rebuild our friendship, as well as come to an agreement about how we want to raise Amber."

"You've got a lot to accomplish," Brant said. "How long will Kaylee and Amber be staying with you?"

"Until the end of October," Colt said, rising to his feet. "And unless I want to do more groveling, I'd better get the crib and other stuff loaded and get back to them."

"Well, congratulations on being a father, little brother," Brant said, standing. "And best of luck with straightening things out with Kaylee."

"Thanks," Colt said, following him into the house. "I have a feeling I'll need all the luck I can get."

Standing in the bedroom she would be sharing with Amber, Kaylee watched Colt as he tried to put the portable crib together with one hand. "I know you like to do things for yourself," she said diplomatically, "but I think you're going to need a little help with that."

"I think you're right." He didn't look happy. "I can't hold it up and lock these braces in place without using both hands."

"I'll support it while you secure it," she said, moving to help him.

"Son of a bi—buck!" Colt stood, slinging his hand.

"What happened?" Kaylee asked, rounding the crib to take his hand in hers. She examined his thumb as she tried to ignore the tingling sensation zinging up her arm. "It doesn't appear to be cut."

He shook his head. "I just pinched the—" he glanced over at Amber sitting in the rocking chair watching them "—heck out of it."

Amber giggled and grabbed the doll Colt had

given her, but didn't hide behind it when she noticed them watching her.

"She thinks you're funny," Kaylee said, smiling fondly at her daughter.

"Do you think Daddy's funny?" Colt asked, grinning at Amber.

When Amber broke into a fresh wave of giggles, Kaylee laughed. "I'd say she finds you very amusing."

"I remember a time when I used to amuse you, too," Colt said, suddenly serious.

Needing to put distance between them, Kaylee tried to release his hand, but his fingers tightened around hers. "That was a long time ago," she said, hating that she sounded so breathless.

"Not that long ago, honey."

When she looked up at his handsome face, his expression caused her heart to stutter. "Colt?"

"Hush," he said, lowering his lips to hers.

Before she could come to her senses and push him away, he released her hand to put his arm around her shoulders and pull her close. Mesmerized by the feel of his firm mouth, his musky male scent and the strength of his hard body pressed to hers, Kaylee didn't even think to protest. Instead her eyes drifted shut and she brought her hands up to rest on his wide chest.

Colt traced her lips, seeking entry to the sensitive recesses beyond, and Kaylee opened for him without hesitation. He touched his tongue to hers to engage her in a game of advance and retreat, sending heat streaking through her veins and making her heart skip several beats. But when he slid his hand down her back to cup her rear, then pull her lower body to his, Kaylee felt as if she'd gone into sensory overload. His burgeoning arousal pressing against her lower stomach, the taste of his passion and the sound of his deep groan made her knees wobble and her head spin. Gripping the front of his denim shirt, she wasn't sure she could keep herself from melting into a puddle at his big, booted feet.

"Mommy, up," Amber said, slapping Kaylee's leg with her little hand. "Up."

Brought back to her senses, Kaylee would have jerked from Colt's embrace, but he held her close as he slowly broke the kiss. "I think a certain little pixie is jealous," he murmured, his words vibrating against Kaylee's lips.

Stepping back, Kaylee shook her head. "That shouldn't have happened."

Colt stared at her for endless seconds and she felt as if she just might drown in the depths of his incredibly blue gaze. "Maybe not, but I'll be da— darned if I'm sorry it did," he finally said.

Kaylee swallowed hard and leaned down to pick up Amber. If she had any sense she'd take her daughter and run as hard and fast as she could back to Oklahoma City.

"Colt, I don't think—"

"Shh, honey," he said, placing his finger to her lips. He stared at her a moment longer, then, turning toward the door, motioned for her to follow him. "I need your help with something else."

Thankful that Amber had interrupted the kiss, Kaylee walked on shaky legs out into the hall. Had she lost her mind? Why had she allowed him to kiss her? Hadn't she learned anything three years ago?

Colt was the man who'd broken her heart. The man who—if she wasn't extremely careful—could do the same thing again.

"I'd like for you to decorate this room for Amber," he said, crossing the hall into another bedroom. Completely empty, the room was like a blank canvas waiting for an artist to bring it to life. "Anything you want to do is fine with me. Buy furniture, wall decorations, toys—whatever you want or need to make it hers."

"Are you sure about this?" Kaylee asked, setting Amber down. She watched her daughter wander around the room as if surveying what was needed to make it comfortable. "That's a lot of expense. We haven't even discussed how often she might be visiting the Lonetree."

"I don't care what it costs," he said, shaking his head. Turning his attention to Amber, he grinned. "I want her to like it."

Kaylee watched his expression as he gazed at

Amber toddling around the room. Colt Wakefield might not have ever loved her, but he certainly cared for their daughter and wanted to do whatever he could to make her happy. He was going to be a wonderful father, and just knowing that caused Kaylee's chest to tighten with emotion.

"Kaylee, are you all right?" Colt asked, sounding concerned. He moved closer to wipe a drop of moisture from her cheek with the pad of his thumb. "What's wrong, honey?"

Unaware that she'd been crying, Kaylee's cheeks burned and she impatiently wiped away her foolish tears. "I—I guess it's just one of those moments when a mother realizes how fast her baby is growing up," she said, hoping her excuse didn't sound as lame to him as it did to her. Needing to put distance between them to collect herself, she started backing from the room. "If you don't mind, I think I'll…see what I can make for supper."

He stared at her curiously. "Sure. Do whatever you like. I want you and Amber to feel like this is your home, too."

Holding a shaky hand out to Amber, Kaylee coaxed, "Come on, sweetie. Let's go downstairs to the kitchen."

Amber looked up with a grin on her face. "Eat."

Colt laughed. "That's my girl. She knows what's important." Smiling, he asked, "Do you think she'd let me watch her while you cook?"

"Maybe," Kaylee said, leading Amber across the loft area of the upper floor. "Do you get the children's television network?"

"I'm pretty sure I do," he said from behind her. "I have a satellite system with about a zillion channels. Surely one of them caters to kids."

"You have that to watch the Rockies baseball games," she said, descending the stairs.

His low chuckle sent a shiver up her spine. "Think you know me pretty well, huh?"

She shrugged as she walked into the kitchen. "At one time I thought I did, but it turned out I was wrong."

He took a step toward her. "Kaylee, we need to talk about—"

"Not now, Colt." She pointed to the entertainment center in the family room. "Why don't you see about tuning in a children's show? Amber might be tempted to watch it with you."

He opened his mouth as if he wanted to argue, then, giving her a short nod, walked into the other room and switched on the big-screen television.

Relieved that he hadn't pressed further, Kaylee breathed a sigh of relief. She wasn't ready to talk about that night three years ago, wasn't sure she ever wanted to hear his reasons for walking away.

As she watched Amber tentatively enter the room where Colt sat, Kaylee bit her lower lip against the deep sadness settling into every cell of her being.

Agreeing to come to the Lonetree with Colt had been a big mistake. For the next couple of months she was going to be with him day-in and day-out, watching him and Amber bond, getting a glimpse of the way life might have been if only Colt could have loved her the way she'd loved him.

Giving herself a mental shake, Kaylee turned to the cabinets and busied herself with finding something to make for supper. What was wrong with her? She'd gotten over him some time ago and had moved on with her life.

But as she peeled potatoes and carrots for a pot roast, she couldn't help but wonder how she was ever going to survive the next couple of months without losing the last scrap of what little sanity she had left.

Five

Colt smiled as he tested the way his shoulder and upper chest felt without the sling. There was a little soreness, but no pain.

"It's about damn time," he muttered.

He tossed the sling on top of the dresser as he walked out of his bedroom and down the hall. As far as he was concerned, he didn't care if he never saw it again. But he knew Kaylee would raise hell with him if he threw it away.

Of course, if she gave him a lecture, it would be an improvement over the silent treatment he'd been getting for the past couple of weeks. Ever since he'd kissed her the day they'd put the crib together she'd been pensive, and although they'd spent a lot of time together, she'd kept her distance both physically and emotionally. He wasn't sure what was running through that pretty little head of hers, but he had every intention of finding out.

The smell of fresh coffee and fried bacon beckoned, and Colt quickened his step. Since Kaylee and Amber arrived, he'd been eating better than he had in ages. At the bottom of the stairs he stepped over the child-safety gate they kept in place to block Amber's access and followed the enticing smell into the kitchen.

"Morning," he said cheerfully as he entered the room. "Something smells mighty good."

"Good morning." Kaylee stopped filling their plates. "Where's your sling?"

"On the dresser in my room," he said, seating himself beside Amber's high chair at the snack bar. He grinned at his daughter and whispered loudly, "Do you think Mommy will yell at Daddy in front of you?"

"Mommy," Amber said, pointing to Kaylee.

"Can you say 'Daddy'?" Colt asked, hoping to hear his daughter use the word for the first time.

Amber nodded her head and picked up a handful of scrambled eggs to put in her spoon.

He and Amber had come a long way. She still wouldn't let him hold her, but she'd stopped hiding her face every time he looked her way and giggled

whenever he talked to her. She'd also started jab-
bering at him. Not a lot. But he suspected as time
went along she'd be a regular little chatterbox.

"No, I'm not going to yell at you," Kaylee said,
placing a heaping plate of eggs, bacon and hash
browns in front of him. She seated herself on the
other side of Amber. "If you say it doesn't hurt,
then it's probably safe to go without the sling." She
handed Amber a sippy cup, then gave him a warning
look. "But if it starts causing you discomfort, you'd
better put the sling back on or I will give you the
talk I give my patients who foolishly try to push for
too much, too soon."

Colt grinned. It wasn't exactly what he'd had in
mind when he decided to draw Kaylee out, but it
was a start. "Yes, ma'am."

"Yes, Mom," Amber repeated.

His daughter's laughter sounded like the tinkling
of a small wind chime on a gentle breeze and he
found himself laughing with her. He loved hearing
her mispronounce words. It was just so darned cute.
Of course, as far as he was concerned, everything
about his little girl was precious.

"Would you two lovely ladies like to join me this
morning for a tour of my part of the Lonetree?" he
asked.

The day after he'd brought them to the ranch the
weather had turned cold as an early winter front had

settled over the area. But today was supposed to be a lot warmer.

"No," Amber said, nodding her head affirmatively.

Colt laughed as he glanced at Kaylee. "Is that a yes or a no?"

Kaylee smiled and he felt like a kid at Christmas. It was the first genuine smile he'd seen from her in quite a while. "I think if you rephrase it so that you're asking if she wants to go outside you might get a more definitive response."

"Would you like for Daddy and Mommy to take you for a walk outside after breakfast, Amber?"

Grinning, the little girl shook her head so hard her raven curls swung back and forth. "Ouside. Now."

"No, sweetie, you have to eat first," Kaylee said gently.

They ate in silence for several minutes before Colt asked, "Have you decided what you're going to do with Amber's room?"

"Not really." Kaylee shrugged one shoulder. "I thought I might do an Internet search to see what's available."

"Good idea." He finished the last bite of his egg, then rose from the bar stool to carry their empty plates to the sink. Rinsing them, he placed them in the dishwasher. "You might even give Annie and

Samantha a call. I'm sure they'd be more than happy to go shopping down in Laramie with you."

"I'll think about it," Kaylee said, wiping Amber's face and hands with a damp cloth, then lifting her from the high chair. "What time did you want to give us that tour?"

"Anytime you're ready."

Taking Amber by the hand, she nodded. "We'll be down as soon I get her changed out of her pajamas."

He watched her lead Amber upstairs. Even though Kaylee had seemed in better spirits this morning, there was a sadness about her that twisted his gut. To know he was the cause of her unhappiness made him feel like the biggest jerk the good Lord ever blessed with the breath of life. How was he going to make things right? What could he do to bring the smile back to Kaylee's pretty face?

She wouldn't allow him to explain why he'd left her alone the morning after he'd made love to her, didn't want to hear his lame excuses. And he couldn't say he blamed her.

For the past few years he'd been telling himself that he was ashamed of taking advantage of her, felt as if he'd betrayed Mitch's trust. But the real reason he'd run like a tail-tucked dog was because of the way Kaylee had made him feel that night. He'd never felt more emotionally connected to another person in his entire life. And it had scared the living hell out of him.

Colt sucked in a sharp breath. Had he been on the verge of falling in love with Kaylee?

He rejected the notion immediately. Emotions had been running high that night, they'd both been hurting from Mitch's loss, and they'd turned to each other for comfort and support.

"You're losing it, Wakefield," he muttered disgustedly.

Shaking his head at his own foolishness, he crossed the great room to the foyer and grabbed his Resistol from one of the hooks by the door. He needed to find a way to make amends for his actions three years ago and to get back the easy friendship he'd once shared with Kaylee, not confuse the issue with a lot of self-analyzation.

"How old is the stallion?" Kaylee asked when Colt walked them over to the enclosed paddock where the black horse she'd seen the day they'd arrived stood munching on a flake of hay.

"He'll be five this spring."

Colt stood so close she could feel the warmth from his much larger body, smell the clean, woodsy scent of his aftershave. Holding Amber's hand, Kaylee stepped closer to the fence to put a little space between them. Her breath caught when he followed her.

"I miss having a horse," she said wistfully.

"What happened to your buckskin mare?"

"I had to sell her at the same time I sold the ranch." It still hurt whenever she thought of having to get rid of the horse Mitch had given her for her twentieth birthday.

"Why did you sell the ranch, Kaylee?" The gentle tone of Colt's deep baritone sent a wave of goose bumps shimmering over her skin.

They hadn't discussed her reasons for selling the ranch. In fact, they hadn't talked about much of anything personal for the past couple of weeks. But telling him why she'd sold the ranch seemed like a safe enough topic.

"I couldn't afford to keep it," she finally said, still hating the fact that she'd had to part with the ranch that her family had owned for more than seventy-five years.

Clearly confused, Colt frowned as he propped his forearms on the top rail of the fence. "But Mitch told me he'd been investing all of his winnings since before your parents died."

"He had been." Turning to face him, she smiled sadly. "Mitch put everything he had into improving the ranch."

"He didn't leave anything in savings?" Colt asked incredulously.

She shook her head. "No. He closed out his account when he started raising Red Brangus cattle."

"He was really proud of that breeding program," Colt said, nodding.

"With good reason." Kaylee stared at a golden eagle tracing lazy circles in the sky above. "But what he didn't tell you, me or anyone else was that he'd not only wiped out his savings, he'd taken a mortgage on the ranch to get the program up and running."

"I had no idea, honey." Colt reached out to cup her cheek and the feel of his calloused palm on her skin sent a tiny spark of electric current to every nerve in her body.

"I didn't, either. I was away at school and didn't find out about any of it until I started going over Mitch's accounts the week after he died." She swallowed around the lump in her throat. Talking about the ranch had been a bad idea, but the conversation had gone too far to turn back now. "Everything would have been fine once he got everything established, but he…died before that happened." Tears flooded her eyes. "And without his PBR winnings to help supplement the ranch, I couldn't keep it going."

"I'm so sorry, honey," Colt said, reaching out to take her into his arms.

Kaylee told herself she should move away, that she needed to put distance between them before she did something stupid. But the feel of his strength surrounding her, the steady beat of his heart beneath her ear, were too comforting to resist.

"Mommy, up," Amber said, tugging on her hand.

Releasing her, Colt bent to pick Amber up, but she pushed his hands away. "No! Mommy."

Kaylee wiped her eyes, then swung her daughter up to hug her close. Amber immediately threw her arms around Kaylee's neck and buried her face in Kaylee's shoulder.

"It's all right, sweetie," Kaylee crooned. "Mommy was just being a big baby and feeling sorry for herself."

"Honey, you have every right—"

"I think I'll take Amber inside now," she interrupted, backing away from him.

Kaylee felt Colt's gaze follow her as she hurried toward the back door. Pride was about all she had left, and she needed time to collect herself before she faced him again. She'd spent three years fighting to keep from lamenting all that she'd lost, and she was embarrassed that he'd seen her give in to it.

Colt watched Kaylee disappear into the house before he let loose with a string of blistering curses, and every single one of them was self-directed. How could he have left her alone to deal with everything she'd had to face after Mitch died? Why hadn't he picked up the phone and at least called to inquire how she was doing?

But as he castigated himself, he knew she would

have never admitted needing help—wouldn't have accepted it from him even if he'd known about her circumstances and offered his assistance. He shook his head. When it came to stubborn pride, Kaylee had enough for a dozen people.

"What the hell were you thinking, Mitch?" he murmured out loud.

The shrill cry of the eagle circling above the pasture had him absently gazing skyward. He couldn't change the past—couldn't bring Mitch back to ask him why he'd left Kaylee without any resources and no recourse but to sell the ranch—and there was no sense spending time wishing that he could.

Staring at the big bird soaring overhead, Colt decided that the past might be over and gone, but the future was a clean slate—wide open and ready for him to start making things easier for Kaylee. In the process he fully intended to see that she was a lot happier than she'd been in a long time.

He grinned suddenly. And he knew exactly where he wanted to start making that happen.

He headed for the house and didn't stop until he was seated behind the desk in his office. Dialing the phone, he didn't bother with a greeting when his oldest brother answered on the third ring.

"Morgan, I need you and Brant to find a buckskin mare for me."

"Colt, I'm only going to tell you this one time," Kaylee said sternly. "If you don't stop trying to push your progress, you're on your own.'' She pointed to the weight room door. ''I'll walk out and you'll have to find someone else to help you with your physical therapy.''

''It won't hurt if I do an extra set of the isometric exercises.'' He frowned. ''Besides, if I don't push myself, I won't be ready in time for finals.''

''I could care less if you make it to Las Vegas,'' she said, unable to stop herself from telling him exactly how she felt. ''I'm not helping you regain the strength in your arm just so you can go back into an arena again and get hurt, or…worse.''

''Calm down, honey,'' he said, taking a step toward her.

''I'm perfectly calm,'' she lied, taking a step back. She wasn't, but he didn't need to know that the very thought of him climbing onto the back of a bull sent a chilling numbness all the way to her very soul. ''I have no intention of helping you risk your life for an eight-second adrenaline rush.''

''You've always known that I'm a bull rider.'' He gave her a measuring look as he advanced. ''Why don't you want me in the arena now, Kaylee?''

She swallowed hard and took another step back. How could she tell him that although she knew they had no future together, she wasn't sure she'd be able to go on if something happened to him?

Before she could think of an excuse without telling him the truth, he walked up to stand in front of her. Placing one finger under her chin, he tipped her face up until their eyes met. "Is it because of what happened to Mitch? Are you afraid something like that will happen to me?"

"Yes…I mean no." Kaylee shook her head. "That's not it at all." She tried putting more distance between them, but she found that he'd backed her up against the wall.

"Which is it, Kaylee?" he asked, gazing down at her from his much taller height. "Does the idea of my getting hurt frighten you?"

"I don't like to see anyone injured," she said evasively.

She suddenly found it hard to take a breath with him so close. Colt had taken his shirt off for the therapy session and the well-developed muscles of his chest and abdomen glistened with a fine sheen of perspiration from the exercises she'd had him doing. She'd never seen him look better.

"You know what I think?" he asked, leaning down to whisper in her ear.

Kaylee shook her head. She couldn't have formed words if her life depended on it.

"I think you're more worried about me than you'd like to admit," he said, his warm breath stirring the hair at her temple. "Whether you like it or not, I think it would matter a great deal to you if I got hurt.'' His lips skimmed the sensitive skin along the column of her neck. ''Am I right, honey?''

She closed her eyes and tried to regain control of her senses. How was she supposed to respond when her heart was racing ninety miles an hour and her knees were threatening to collapse?

When his arms closed around her, Kaylee's eyes flew open and she brought her hands up to his chest to push him away. ''C-Colt, I—''

''It's okay, honey,'' he said a moment before his mouth descended to hers. ''All I'm going to do is kiss you.''

From the first featherlight touch of his lips on hers, Kaylee was lost. If she'd had the ability to think, she might have protested, but feeling his strong arms surround her, the warmth of his hard, muscled chest beneath her palms, and she was lucky to remember her own name.

Her eyes drifted shut, and as he coaxed her to open for him, the last traces of her will to resist dissipated like mist beneath the rays of a warm summer sun. She knew she was playing a dangerous game, but as Colt's tongue stroked hers, her body tingled to life and she shamelessly melted against him. She wanted to taste him, wanted to once again experience the thrill of his kiss.

Her heart pounded and her breathing became shallow as he explored her thoroughly, eliciting responses from her that she'd kept buried for three long years. When he brought one hand up to cup her breast, the sensation of his thumb chafing her hardened nipple through the layers of her clothing caused her stomach to flutter and deep need to pool in the pit of her stomach. No other man had ever made her feel the way Colt did, never caused her to lose the ability to think straight.

He shifted his hips and the feel of his arousal sent heat streaking through her with an intensity that robbed her of breath. He wanted her as she wanted him.

The realization that her feelings for Colt could very easily come back full-force hit like a physical blow and helped to clear her head. If she didn't put a halt to things, and very quickly, she was in danger of making a fool of herself. Hadn't past experience taught her that the physical desire he had for her wasn't the same as an emotional bond?

The thought brought back some of her sanity and she whimpered as she pushed against him. She couldn't—wouldn't—allow herself to fall for him again.

"Please…Colt. Let me go."

He leaned back to stare at her. "We need to talk."

Kaylee shook her head as she pulled from his arms. "I have to get Amber up from her nap. Annie called this morning and asked if we would go shopping with her."

He caught her by the arm. "You're going to have to listen to me sometime, Kaylee."

Looking down at his strong hand holding her captive, she pried his fingers from her wrist and stepped away from him. "There's really no point, Colt." She turned toward the door. "We've never been on the same page, and I seriously doubt we ever will be."

Colt watched her walk from the room, head high, her damnable pride wrapped around her like some kind of protective armor. How the hell was he going to get through to her? How could he explain about that night three years ago if she wouldn't listen to him?

He sat heavily on the weight bench and stared off into space. What he needed was Kaylee's undivided attention. But how was he going to get that?

The only time they were alone was when Amber took a nap, and Kaylee insisted on conducting his therapy sessions during that time. He'd tried a couple of times over the past week to talk to her while she put him through the exercises, but each time she'd turned into a no-nonsense physical trainer with all the personality of an army drill sergeant.

Short of putting a gag in her mouth and tying her up, Colt didn't have any idea how he was going to get her to listen to him.

"You look like your mind is about a million miles

away, Colt. Is something wrong?'' his sister-in-law Annie asked from the doorway.

Looking up, Colt started to shake his head, but ended up nodding instead. ''I've got a hell of a problem and her name is Kaylee.''

Annie gave him an inquisitive look. ''Anything I can do to help?''

Colt blew out a frustrated breath. ''You wouldn't happen to have some rope and a gag with you?''

''No, those aren't items I normally carry around in my purse,'' she said dryly. She walked over to sit beside him on the weight bench. ''Although, come to think of it, there are times when I could use them on your brother to get him to listen to me.''

''He is a stubborn cuss, isn't he?'' Colt asked, grinning.

''No more so than you and Morgan.'' Annie smiled. ''Now, what can I do to help?''

''Do you and Brant have plans for tomorrow night?'' he asked as an idea began to take shape.

To Colt's relief Annie shook her head. ''No. Brant doesn't have a rodeo or PBR event scheduled this weekend, so we're free. What do you need us to do?''

''I think Kaylee could use a night out. Would you and Brant bring Zach over and watch Amber while Kaylee and I go down to Laramie?''

Annie smiled. ''Sure. I'll call Morgan and Samantha and have them bring Timmy and Jared over, too. I think it's time the Wakefield cousins got to know each other.''

Colt nodded. ''Could you keep this under your hat while you and Kaylee are out shopping today? I'd like to surprise her.''

''Are you sure about this?'' Annie looked skeptical. ''Take it from me. Women like a little advanced notice when they're being taken out on a date.''

He shook his head. ''This isn't a date.''

She gave him a knowing smile. ''Whatever you say, Colt.'' She rose to her feet when they heard Kaylee and Amber coming downstairs. ''Where are you taking her?''

Where was he taking Kaylee?

''Probably out to eat,'' he finally said. ''And maybe a movie.''

His sister-in-law grinned. ''If that isn't a date, what would you call it?''

''I—'' He stopped to consider what he would call his night out with Kaylee. ''I'm not sure, but it's definitely not a date.''

When he followed Annie into the great room, he watched Kaylee smile and reach to hug his sister-in-law. ''It's so good to see you again, Annie.''

''It's good to see you, too,'' Annie said, hugging Kaylee back. She bent down. ''And you must be Amber.''

Grinning, Amber nodded and held up her arms for Annie to pick her up.

Envy stabbed Colt's gut when Annie picked up his daughter. In the three weeks since he'd found out about her, Amber had gotten to where she jabbered at him and laughed at just about everything he did, but still wouldn't allow him to hold her.

As Kaylee gathered her purse and jacket, the two women started talking about making a stop at Baby World so Annie could look at something called a layette for the baby she was expecting in a couple of months. Fishing his wallet from the hip pocket of his jeans, Colt held his credit card out to Kaylee.

"Buy whatever you want or need." When she started to refuse, he hurried to add, "If you find the furniture you want for Amber's room go ahead and buy it. I'll drive down tomorrow to pick it up."

Kaylee finally took the plastic card from him, but he noticed that she was careful to keep from touching his fingers. "Hopefully they'll have a sale," she said, tucking it into her shoulder bag.

He shrugged. "Doesn't matter to me what it costs. Get whatever you like."

Annie set Amber on her feet. "Are you ready to go spend your daddy's money, Amber?"

"Daddy," Amber said, nodding and pointing at him.

Colt's chest tightened, and he couldn't have stopped his ear-to-ear grin, nor could he have strung two words together to save his own life. It was the first time his little girl had called him "Daddy," and he couldn't believe what an incredible feeling it gave him.

Six

"Colt, keep your elbow straight and your shoulder elevated so that your arm is parallel to the floor," Kaylee said, stepping close. "Now bring it across your body."

Taking hold of his arm to lift it to the proper position, she did her best to ignore how hard his bicep was, how being so close to him affected her breathing. She quickly placed one end of a long narrow strip of thin rubber in his left hand, then took the other end and stood at his right side.

"Keeping your arm straight, pull this back as far as you can without pain," she instructed.

"That should be easy," he said, testing the stretchy band.

When he actually started the exercise, Kaylee noticed him wince when he had the band stretched almost even with his shoulder. "That's far enough. Now, slowly let it retract." She waited until he had returned his arm to the rest position. "Next time, don't go quite as far as you went the last time. I don't want you experiencing any pain."

"No pain, no gain," he said, pulling on the rubber again.

When she noticed sweat popping out on his forehead and a muscle jerk along his lean jaw, she calmly took the band from his hand and started for the door. "That's it."

"Hey, I wasn't finished," he said, frowning. "You told me I needed to do two sets of ten. I only finished seven out of the first set."

She spun around to face him. "I also told you to stop before you felt any kind of pain."

"It didn't hurt that much," he insisted, his expression belligerent.

Anger swept through her and, stepping forward, she poked his bare chest with her finger. "Look, Mr. Macho Cowboy, I told you absolutely no pain. What part of that statement don't you understand?"

He picked up a towel to wipe the perspiration from his forehead. "I understand it fine. I just don't happen to agree with it."

"Then you'll have to find another P.T." She

walked down the short hall to the great room before he caught up with her.

"I don't want another physical therapist," he said, taking her by the upper arm.

She looked down at his big hand, then met his determined gaze head-on. "I don't work with patients who refuse to follow my instructions."

They stared at each other for several long seconds in a silent battle of wills before he finally nodded and let go of her arm. "All right. I'll do what you say, but only on one condition."

"*You're* going to set conditions?" She laughed at his audacity. "You certainly are a piece of work, aren't you?"

His charming grin sent her pulse into overdrive. "Yeah, but that's what you've always liked about me."

"Give me a break," she said, rolling her eyes. "So what's the condition?"

"I want you to go down to Laramie with me to pick up Amber's furniture this afternoon," he said earnestly. "We'll leave around five."

She looked at her watch. "By the time we get finished with your exercises it's going to be too late. The store will be closed before we could get there."

He shook his head. "I called earlier. Baby World doesn't close until eight on Friday nights."

"But I really should stay here and—"

"Please?"

He looked so hopeful, she found herself nodding

before she could stop herself. "All right. But remember your end of the bargain."

"What's that?" he asked, frowning.

She lightly tapped his shoulder with her finger. "No pain."

"Oh, yeah." He grinned. "Not a problem."

Kaylee thought he'd given in a little too easily, but she didn't have time to wonder about it when the sound of her daughter waking from her nap came from the baby monitor clipped to her belt. "I'll go get Amber and be back down to finish your strengthening exercises."

"Why don't we knock off for today?" he asked, draping the towel around his neck.

She narrowed her eyes. "You just spent the last ten minutes arguing with me about how you want to push yourself, and now you want to quit for the day?" She frowned. "Are you in pain?"

He laughed as they started up the stairs. "Nope. I just thought you might want to start getting ready to go out."

When she stopped dead in her tracks, he bumped into her from behind. A sizzling thrill ran from the top of her head to the soles of her feet. Quickly putting distance between them, she turned to face him. "We're just going to pick up a youth bed, mattress and chest. This isn't a date."

"Nope." He shook his head. "It's definitely not a date."

*   *   *

"If this isn't a date, Colt Wakefield, what would you call it?"

Colt glanced at Kaylee from the corner of his eye as he steered the truck onto the main highway toward Laramie. He didn't think he'd ever seen her quite this angry. But at least she was talking to him again. It sure as hell beat the dead silence he'd endured from the time Brant, Annie and Zach had shown up to watch Amber. For a few minutes when they'd first arrived, Colt hadn't been sure Kaylee wouldn't refuse to go with him.

"It's just a night out," he said calmly.

Maybe Annie was right. Maybe women didn't like being surprised about things like this.

"You set this up, didn't you?" Kaylee accused. "It wasn't just a coincidence that Annie and Brant dropped by as we were getting ready to leave."

Setting the cruise control, he leaned back for the hour's drive to Laramie before he answered her. "I'm not going to lie to you. I did arrange for them to watch Amber this evening." He checked his watch, "And by now, Morgan, Samantha and their boys are there, too."

She glared at him across the truck cab. "Why?"

"Because I thought you could use a break," he answered honestly. "You've been busy cooking and helping me with therapy, and I wanted to show my appreciation. That's why I decided to treat you to supper and a movie.''

''Don't you think it would have been more considerate to ask me, instead of arranging everything first?'' She still sounded irritated, but not quite as angry as she had only moments before.

''I wanted to surprise you,'' he said defensively. He purposely failed to mention that he'd known she wouldn't have gone otherwise.

''You certainly achieved your goal. I feel like I've been blindsided.'' She gazed out the passenger window for several long seconds before she spoke again. ''Could you promise me something, Colt?''

''What's that, honey?'' he asked, tensing. From the tone of her voice, he wasn't sure he wanted to hear what she was about to ask of him.

''Please, don't play games with me. I've never been good at them.''

The emotion he detected in her quietly spoken request had him disengaging the cruise control and steering the truck to the shoulder of the road. He killed the engine, then turned to look at her. She was staring down at her hands, which were clasped tightly in her lap.

''Kaylee, look at me.'' When she shook her head, he cupped her chin and gently turned her head until their gazes met. ''I give you my word, I'm not playing games. A lot has happened in the past three weeks and I thought you could use a little time to relax.'' The feel of her satiny skin against his calloused palm quickly had his temperature rising. Dropping his hand to keep from pulling her into his arms, he took a deep breath. ''Tonight is about two old friends getting together to catch up and have a few laughs. That's all.''

She stared at him a moment longer, then, looking resigned, she nodded. ''All right. But I'd like to get back to your place early. I know Amber is satisfied with Annie watching her, and she's going to love playing with Zach, and Morgan's boys, but she's used to me putting her to bed. She might be frightened if I'm not there.''

''That works for me,'' he said, starting the truck and pulling back onto the road. It wasn't the evening he'd planned, but he'd take what he could get. ''We'll pick up the furniture, then stop at the Broken Spoke Steakhouse on the way back.''

''Is that the place offering a free meal to everyone at the table if one person orders and manages to eat their biggest steak?'' she asked, sounding a little more relaxed.

''That's the one. It's a thirty-two ounce piece of prime Black Angus beef. But the kicker is, you have to eat a huge pile of fries along with it. Whenever Mitch came home with me, we'd stop there.'' Colt chuckled. ''And they lost money on the deal every time.''

''It doesn't surprise me,'' she said, shaking her

head. "Mitch was a bottomless pit. He could eat more than any person I've ever known."

Colt grinned. "It amazed me that he never gained weight."

"I know," she said, laughing. "I used to think that was so unfair. Mitch ate like a horse and stayed thin, while I dieted and gained weight."

When their laughter faded, Colt stared at the road ahead. "Mitch and I had a lot of good times over the years."

"He really loved you, Colt," she said quietly. "You were like a brother to him."

Colt's gut clenched painfully, as it always did when he thought of losing the best friend he'd ever had. "I felt the same way about him."

They rode in silence for several miles as Colt wrestled with his conscience. He wasn't sure if he was about to ruin what little friendship they had left, but they needed to clear the air about what happened three years ago.

"Kaylee, I know you don't want to talk about it, but I think it's time we stopped walking on eggshells around each other, talk over what happened the morning after we made love, and move on."

Her quick intake of breath was the only sound she made for several tense moments. "I'm not sure I can do that, Colt." Her voice shook and he could tell this wasn't going to be easy for either of them.

"We have to, honey," he said, reaching over to

take her hand in his. "We have a little girl depending on us to work this out between us. Her happiness depends on it."

Kaylee remained silent so long, he wasn't sure she was going to agree. "All right," she finally said, sighing. "Say what you feel you have to and get it over with."

He stared at the road ahead as he tried to put his thoughts into words. "First off, I want you to know there hasn't been a day gone by that I haven't regretted the way I handled the situation." Taking a deep breath, he figured it was better to say it outright and get it over with. "I left without waking you that morning because I was so ashamed of what I'd done, I couldn't face you, Kaylee. I know it was the coward's way out, but I knew I couldn't stand seeing the regret or the hatred in your eyes for what I'd done."

"What on earth gave you the impression that I'd feel that way?" She sounded shocked.

"Because you turned to me for comfort and I let things go too far." He swallowed down his own self-disgust. "I should have called a halt to things before it got out of hand."

"Excuse me? What makes you think you were the only one who could have stopped what happened?" she asked incredulously. She shook her head. "Let me clue you in on something, cowboy. You weren't alone in that bed. I could have—"

"No, Kaylee." He heard what she was saying, but he couldn't let her take any part of the blame for what had happened. "Mitch was my best friend, and the night after his funeral I was taking his sister's virginity." Colt shook his head. "Do you really think that's something I'm proud of?"

She reached out to put her hand on his arm. "Colt—"

"If I could go back and change things, I swear I would, Kaylee," he said seriously.

They remained silent for some time before she spoke again. "There's something that I wouldn't change about what happened three years ago even if I could," she said quietly.

"What's that, honey?"

There was no hesitation when she answered. "Amber. She's my life now."

Colt swallowed hard as he digested what Kaylee had just told him. She didn't regret having his child. Did that mean she had no regrets about making love with him?

"I have to ask you something, and I want you to be completely honest with me," he said, his heart pumping so hard he wasn't sure she couldn't hear it.

"I think we've gone over—"

"I wouldn't ask if it wasn't important to me, Kaylee," he said, taking her hand in his.

She looked as if she was going to refuse, then finally nodded. "All right. What do you want to know?"

"You said you weren't sorry you had Amber." He took a deep breath. He'd probably gone completely around the bend, but he had to know. "Do you have any regrets about making love with me that night?"

She remained silent a moment, then shook her head. "No. I've never been sorry about what happened that night."

Two hours later, as they left the Broken Spoke Steakhouse and turned onto the road leading back to the Lonetree, Colt was still thinking about Kaylee's admission. Hell, he hadn't been able to think of anything else the entire evening.

Had he been wrong all this time about what happened that night?

For three years he'd convinced himself that he'd taken advantage of her, that he'd seduced her when she'd been the most vulnerable. But had that really been the case? Or had she been just as desperate as he'd been to escape the emotional trauma of losing Mitch with the life-affirming act of making love with someone she really cared for?

"Colt, are you all right?" Kaylee asked, dragging his attention back to the present.

He shook off his disturbing speculation as he glanced at her across the truck cab. "Sure. Why do you ask?"

"You've been distracted all evening," she said, looking concerned. "And when we were eating, you kept staring at your steak like you expected it to moo. I've never known you to lose your appetite before."

"Well, it was pretty rare."

"It was definitely that," Kaylee said, grinning.

The appearance of her smile and the sound of her velvet voice caused his heart to thump hard against his ribs. He didn't think he'd ever seen her look prettier, or more desirable.

But he was determined to keep things light. He wasn't willing to jeopardize the easy mood that had developed between them over the course of the evening.

"Did you enjoy yourself tonight?" he asked as he casually stretched his arm along the back of the bench seat.

"Yes, I did." She hesitated a moment before she added, "But I owe you an apology."

"For what?" He couldn't think of anything that she'd need to apologize for.

"I'm sorry for the way I acted earlier," she said,

her voice small. "You know, about your surprising me this evening."

Her silky hair brushed his hand, sending tiny currents of electricity streaking through him. He couldn't stop himself from tangling his fingers in the auburn strands.

"I'm just glad you had a good time, honey."

"But I shouldn't have overreacted the way I did," she insisted. "You were just trying to be nice and—"

"I think we both learned something about each other tonight," he interrupted.

She turned her head to give him a questioning look. "What would that be?"

"I'm not nearly as devious as you thought." He chuckled as he steered the truck onto the lane leading to his house. "And you don't like surprises."

She shook her head. "That's not entirely true. It depends on the surprise." Grinning, she added, "Sometimes they can be very nice."

Parking the truck, he got out and walked around to open the passenger door for her. "I'll remind you of that the next time I decide to surprise you."

Even though she was smiling, she looked a bit apprehensive. "Next time?"

"Sure." When she got out of the truck, he shut the door then draped a companionable arm across her shoulders and started walking toward the house. "Didn't you know, life is nothing more than a series of astounding events, punctuated by stretches of monotonous boredom?''

"That's pretty deep for a cowboy," she said, laughing.

"Watch it, brat." He gave her a playful hug as he pressed a kiss to the top of her head. "I'll have you know I made straight A's in my college philosophy courses."

"You actually attended classes?" She shook her head in mock amazement. "I'm impressed. I always thought you and Mitch were there to meet girls."

"Well, there was that, too," he said, grinning. As they climbed the porch steps, he chuckled. "But there's a funny thing about those scholarships they give out for college rodeo teams."

"What's that?"

"They actually expect you to pass a few classes."

"Imagine that," she said laughing.

Reluctant for the evening to end, when they reached the front door Colt turned her to face him. "I know that you don't like surprises," he said, using his thumb to push his hat back on his head. With the brim out of the way, he took her into his arms. "So I think I'd better warn you. I'm going to kiss you now, Kaylee."

She gazed up at him, and just when he thought she was going to tell him to buzz off, she nodded. "I think I'd like that, Colt."

Lowering his head, he told himself to keep the

kiss simple. But the moment his mouth touched hers, the spark of desire that had been flickering inside him all evening ignited into a flame. He couldn't have stopped himself from pulling her to him any more than he could stop the changing of the seasons.

When her lips parted on a soft sigh and he slipped his tongue inside, the sweet taste that was uniquely Kaylee made his pulse pound and his temperature soar. As he stroked her tongue with his, a tiny moan escaped her and she put her arms around his neck. The feel of her nails lightly raking the sensitive skin at his nape and her eagerness to get closer to him sent shock waves to every cell in his body and liquid fire racing through his veins.

Her supple body molding to his quickly worked its magic and his arousal was not only predictable, it made him light-headed with its intensity. Sliding one hand down to cup her delightful little bottom, he pulled her forward. He wanted her to feel the need she'd created in him, to let her know how wrong she'd been about his not being attracted to her.

Bringing his other hand up under her jean jacket and along her side, he cupped her breast and chafed her puckered nipple through the layers of her pink T-shirt and bra. The bud tightened further and his own body hardened in response. He'd never wanted a woman more than he wanted Kaylee at that very moment.

Slowly breaking the kiss, he held her close as he tried to bring his breathing under control. How on God's green earth had he managed to talk himself into believing that he and Kaylee could return to the easy relationship they'd once shared?

Hell, nothing could be further from the truth. With sudden clarity, Colt realized that he and Kaylee had crossed a line three years ago and there was no turning back. The only thing they could do now would be to move forward and try to build something new.

"Colt, I…we—" She shook her head. "This can't happen again."

"It's all right, honey."

Easing back, Colt found the sight of her perfect lips slightly swollen from his kiss and the rosy blush of desire on her pale cheeks absolutely fascinating. Her luminous violet eyes were filled with questions that at the moment he couldn't even begin to answer. And he wasn't fool enough to try.

"Don't be frightened of what's happening between us, Kaylee." He smoothed her silky auburn hair with a shaky hand. "We're not going to rush into something before we're both ready. This time we're going to take it a step at a time and see where it leads us." He kissed the tip of her cute little nose. "Now, let's go inside and listen to my brothers and their wives tell us how adorable our daughter is and how much fun she had getting to know her cousins.''

As Kaylee gazed up at Colt, she knew beyond a shadow of doubt that her feelings for him were as strong, if not stronger, than they had ever been. The realization caused her breathing to stall and her heart to skip several beats. .

For the past few years she'd convinced herself that she'd gotten over him, that she'd moved on with her life. But it was past time she stopped lying to herself and faced the truth. She'd never stopped loving Colt—could never stop loving him.

She bit her lower lip against the panic threatening to swamp her. But before she had the chance to come to grips with her discovery and what it might mean to her sanity, Colt stepped back, took her hand in his and opened the front door.

Dazed and feeling as if she was moving through a heavy fog, she allowed him to lead her through the house to the family room. Standing just inside the doorway, she watched Amber put her arms around a baby boy, who appeared to be about a year old, as she kissed his chubby little cheek.

''Baby,'' she said, grinning at Annie and another woman sitting on the couch.

When the woman Kaylee assumed to be Morgan's wife, Samantha, turned to smile at Amber, she noticed Kaylee and Colt. ''Look who's home, Amber.''

"Mommy!" Amber said, her grin widening as she ran over for Kaylee to pick her up.

"Did you have a good time with your cousins?" Kaylee asked, swinging her daughter up into her arms.

"No," Amber said, nodding affirmatively. She immediately began to wiggle as she pointed to the floor. "Down."

"Hey there, Kaylee-Q," Brant said as he and Morgan both rose from their chairs. He wrapped her in a bear hug. "It's good to see you again."

"It's nice seeing you, too, Brant," she said, meaning it.

She'd missed seeing Colt's brothers. They'd always treated her and Mitch like they were members of their family.

When Brant released her, Morgan took his place. "It's been way too long, Kaylee. We've missed having you around."

She hugged the oldest of the Wakefield brothers. "You've just missed having someone around to tease unmercifully."

"I see you can still hold your own with us," Morgan said, laughing as he released her. He held out his arm for the pretty, brown-haired woman to step into his embrace. "Kaylee, this is my wife, Samantha."

"It's nice to finally meet you, Kaylee," Samantha said, smiling. "I've heard so much about you, I feel like I've known you for years. In fact, Annie and I were just talking about taking you with us down to Laramie next week for lunch and shopping.''

Annie grinned. ''We thought a girls' afternoon at the mall would be nice.''

''I'd like that,'' Kaylee said, noticing Brant and Morgan simultaneously wink and grin at their wives as if they shared a delightful secret.

Before she had a chance to speculate on what was going on, a little boy walked over to them and held his arms up to Colt. ''Unca Colt, I gots a new watch like the rangers on TV wear.''

''You sure do, Timmy,'' Colt said, picking the child up to sit on his right forearm.

''No,'' Amber said shaking her head vigorously.

Shocked at the uncharacteristic vehemence in her daughter's voice and the correct use of the negative gesture, Kaylee turned to watch Amber run across the room toward the adults. When she stopped in front of Colt, she held up her little arms for him to pick her up.

''Up, Daddy,'' Amber insisted. ''Up.''

Seven

Colt's heart stopped then took off at a gallop at Amber's insistence that he pick her up. It was the first time his daughter had wanted him to hold her and he wasn't about to miss the opportunity. Unfortunately, he still couldn't lift anything with his left arm, and if he set Timmy on his feet, Colt ran the risk of hurting the little boy's feelings. And that was something he just wouldn't do.

"Let me take him," Morgan said, apparently sensing Colt's dilemma.

"Thanks," Colt said, handing the three-year-old to his dad.

With his right arm free, he bent to lift his daughter

up to sit on his forearm. She immediately wrapped her little arms around his neck to give him a hug before she turned to glare at Timmy.

"Mine Daddy," she said as if staking her claim.

Colt's chest tightened with emotion and he felt as if he had a lump the size of a basketball clogging his throat. The feeling of finally holding his daughter, of knowing that she'd accepted him, was overwhelming.

He felt Kaylee touch his elbow. Being careful not to move his shoulder farther than was comfortable, he put his left arm around her waist and pulled her to his side. Gazing down at her, he suddenly felt as if he held everything in his arms that he'd ever wanted. It should have scared the hell out of him. Instead, it filled him with a sense of completion like nothing he'd ever known.

Unaware that she'd given Colt a moment he'd never forget as long as he lived, Amber began to pull on the wide brim of his hat. "Me wear. Me."

He couldn't have denied her if his life depended on it. Removing his Resistol, he set it on her little head so that it didn't cover her eyes. "There you go, pixie."

"I think Amber is going to be a Daddy's girl," Annie said as she wiped a tear from her cheek.

"I think so, too," Samantha agreed, sniffling. When Colt's youngest nephew, Jared, whimpered and lifted his arms for his mother to pick him up,

Samantha smiled. "I hate to cut the evening short, but I think we need to take the boys home and get them ready for bed."

Annie nodded. "Brant and I need to do the same with Zach."

"Come on, partner," Brant said, catching his son around the waist to swing the little boy up and onto his shoulders. "Mommy said it's time for us to head home."

Colt held his daughter as he and Kaylee walked his brothers and their families to the door. "Thanks for watching Amber this evening."

"It was our pleasure," Samantha said, raising on tiptoe to kiss Amber's cheek. "Bye-bye, Amber."

Amber raised her hand and waved, then laid her head on Colt's shoulder. The gesture was so trusting that he thought his heart might burst from the love filling it.

"You have a sweet little girl there, Colt," Morgan said. Turning to Kaylee, he smiled. "If this joker gives you any problems, don't hesitate to call me. I'll straighten him out in a hurry."

"And if you can't get hold of Morgan, call me," Brant added with a grin.

"Thanks for the votes of confidence," Colt grumbled as he watched Kaylee accept hugs from both of his brothers.

"I'll call you tomorrow about our afternoon at the

mall, Kaylee,'' Annie said before giving Colt a knowing grin.

Now what was that all about?

He'd noticed the bemused expressions on both of his brothers' and their wives' faces each time the trip to the mall had been mentioned. But before he could ask what was going on, Annie gave Amber a little wave, then hurried across the porch and down the steps.

When he closed the door behind his family, he turned to see Kaylee watching him. She looked a bit uncertain, and he knew she was mulling over what he'd said about them taking things slowly.

"Kaylee, I—"

"I think it's time this little lady got ready for bed,'' she said, interrupting him. She held out her hands to take Amber. "It's been a big evening.''

Realizing that Kaylee was talking about herself as much as she was Amber, Colt hugged and kissed Amber's baby soft cheek. "Sleep tight, pixie.'' Reluctantly handing her to Kaylee, he asked, "Do you need help?''

Kaylee shook her head. "She's normally easy to get to sleep.'' Starting toward the stairs, she turned back. "I'm, um, pretty tired. I think I'll turn in for the night, too. Thank you for the evening out. I'll see you at breakfast tomorrow morning. Good night.''

"'Night,'' Colt said, watching Kaylee hurry up the stairs with Amber.

He shook his head when she disappeared down the hall. Kaylee needed time to come to the same conclusion he'd reached earlier in the evening. They would never—could never—be "just" friends. Thinking back on it, he wasn't sure they ever had been.

Kaylee handed Colt a small weight. "I'm going to warn you before we start the next phase of your therapy, I won't tolerate your trying to lift anything heavier than this. Understand?"

"I can lift more than this thing with my little finger," he said, testing the three-pound weight in his left hand.

"You'd better not," she said sternly. She knew if she didn't lay down the law now, he would push for more and end up reinjuring himself.

"Aw, come on, honey. I know I can lift twice this much." His charming grin caused her pulse to take off at breakneck speed. "The least you can do is let me try."

She hardened herself to his supplicating expression and shook her head. "Not until we see if doing the biceps curls are going to bother you."

"They won't."

"Do three sets of ten with these weights, then we'll talk," she said, refusing to budge.

He stared at her with narrowed eyes as if trying to intimidate her. Fortunately she wasn't that easily coerced.

"Oh, all right," he finally said, glaring at her as he plopped onto the weight bench.

Watching him begin the exercise, Kaylee tried to remind herself that he was like any other patient she'd worked with. But she knew she was only fooling herself. Colt could never be just another person to her. Ever.

If she hadn't known that before, she would have after last night. He'd kissed her before, but never like he had after they returned home from their evening in Laramie. When he'd pressed his lips to hers, then deepened the kiss, it had felt as if fireworks had been ignited in her soul. And if that hadn't been enough to convince her, what he'd told her afterward certainly would have. He'd said not to be afraid of what was happening between them, that they were going to take things slowly and not rush into anything they weren't ready for this time.

This time.

Two very simple little four-letter words with the power to scare her as little else could. She shivered at the thought of what they implied.

Colt had indicated, in a roundabout way, that he wanted them to explore a relationship that went well beyond friendship. But could she do that? Would she be able to survive if it didn't work out for them?

Three years ago, the only thing that had kept her going after losing her brother and having Colt walk away had been Amber. Kaylee had focused on her pregnancy, then after Amber's birth, she'd concentrated all of her energy into being the best mother she could be. And it had worked. She'd picked up the pieces of her life and moved on because Colt hadn't been around to remind her that she'd put her heart on the line and lost.

But this time, everything would be different. Now that he knew about their daughter, Kaylee would see him on a regular basis when he came to visit Amber.

And what would happen if things *did* work out between them? Would she be able to accept what he did for a living?

When she'd lost Mitch to the sport of bull riding, she'd lost her only living relative, and it had very nearly been the end of her. But how would she survive if something happened to Colt? The thought was so frightening she had to wrap her arms around herself to ward off the chill.

"Kaylee, are you okay?"

When she glanced up, she was surprised to see that Colt was standing right in front of her. "Y-yes, I'm fine. I was…thinking about the next phase of your therapy," she lied.

He stared at her a moment before shaking his head. "No you weren't." Tracing his finger down her cheek, he gave her a smile so tender that her toes curled inside her cross-trainers. "We both need to stop dancing around what we're really thinking, Kaylee. Being up front and honest with each other is the only way we're going to have a chance of making it work out this time around." He leaned forward to lightly brush her lips with his. "And I want that chance, honey."

A shiver of longing coursed through her at his touch. "Really, I was just—"

She stopped abruptly to stare into his brilliant blue eyes. He was right. If they were going to attempt a relationship, it had to be based on complete honesty. She'd already admitted to herself that she still cared for him—had never stopped caring for him—but did she have the courage to tell him? Did she dare open herself up to the possibility of more heartbreak?

"What do *you* want, Kaylee?" he asked, his voice gentle. "Tell me what's really going on in that pretty little head of yours."

Staring up at him, she knew what she wanted— what she had always wanted. "I-I'm afraid, Colt."

He immediately wrapped her in his arms and pulled her to his wide chest. "Honey, I know it's scary. But anything worth having is always risky." His hands caressed her with a reverence that brought tears to her eyes. "And we'll never know what we could have together if we don't give it a try."

The feel of his strength surrounding her, the soothing sound of his deep baritone and the steady

beat of his heart beneath her ear gave her the courage she needed to tell him what was in her heart.
''The thought of failing scares me to death, but I'm
even more frightened of never knowing what we
could have together.'' Leaning back to look up into
his handsome face, she took a deep breath. ''Yes,
Colt. I'd like to see where this leads us.''

As Colt flipped through the channels, Amber sat
up in his lap and pointed at the television. ''Mato!''

''You want to watch this?'' he asked as an animated tomato and cucumber scooted across the
screen.

''Yes, yes, yes,'' she said as she shook her head
in a negative gesture.

''Okay, pixie,'' he said, kissing the top of her
head and settling back in his recliner. ''We'll watch
this until Mommy says it's time for you to go to
bed.''

He frowned as he watched the vegetables sing,
dance and crack jokes. Cartoons sure had changed
a lot since he was a little kid. Whatever happened
to the good old days when cars, trucks and airplanes
transformed into robots, or lions, tigers and panthers
talked and fought skeleton-like villains?

But several minutes later, Colt found himself
laughing out loud at a talking stalk of broccoli.
''This is pretty good stuff, pixie.''

Giggling, Amber scrambled up his chest, placed

her little hands on his cheeks and gave him a sloppy baby kiss.

"How are you two doing?" Kaylee asked, walking into the family room from the kitchen.

"I can see now why you decorated Amber's room with these characters," Colt said, grinning. "She loves this show."

"From the way you were laughing, I think you're getting just as big of a kick out of it," Kaylee said, smiling back at him.

Colt swallowed hard. How in the name of Sam Hill was he going to keep his hands to himself if she kept turning that killer smile on him?

After their talk this afternoon, he'd told himself it was more important than ever for them not to rush into anything. They needed to let their feelings for each other build slowly in order to be certain that when they made love it was right for both of them.

But now he wasn't sure that was going to be an option. Not when he found everything Kaylee said, every move she made, sexy as hell. And just knowing they would eventually be exploring the chemistry that had always simmered between them was enough to keep him in a constant state of arousal.

"Colt, did you hear me?" she asked, picking up Amber.

He shook his head. "Sorry, I was thinking about something I need…to do."

"I asked if you would mind watching Amber on

Monday morning while I go to the mall with Annie and Samantha,'' Kaylee said patiently.

"Sure." Turning the television off, he rose from the chair. "But I thought you were supposed to go some afternoon."

Kaylee nodded. "We were. But Annie has an early doctor's appointment and wondered if Samantha and I would like to go shopping afterward and then have lunch."

When she started toward the stairs, he followed her. "Do you want to take my credit card?"

"No."

"Wait a minute," he said, taking hold of her arm. He removed his wallet from his hip pocket. "I want you to get some more stuff for Amber's room."

"What kind of *stuff?*" she asked, frowning as she accepted the plastic card.

He shrugged. "Toys, stuffed animals, clothes, whatever you think she'd like." Leaning down, he kissed Amber's cheek. "Sleep tight, little pixie." He brushed Kaylee's lips with his, then added, "After you get her to bed, come back downstairs."

The phone rang before she could answer. "You'd better get that while I get Amber into bed," she said, turning to go upstairs.

Cursing the caller's timing, Colt watched Kaylee's delightful little bottom as she climbed the stairs. When the phone rang for the third time, he marched into his office and snatched the cordless unit from its base. "What?"

"Did I interrupt something, little brother?" Morgan asked without missing a beat.

Colt blew out a frustrated breath. "Did anyone ever tell you how lousy your timing is?"

Morgan's hearty laughter echoed in Colt's ear. "I seem to remember Brant saying something similar the first time he brought Annie to the Lonetree."

"Well, he was right," Colt said, his anger over the interruption beginning to cool. "What's up, bro?"

"I've got some news about that buckskin mare you wanted me and Brant to find."

Colt perked up immediately. "Is she for sale?"

"Not anymore," Morgan said, sounding quite pleased. "Unless, of course, *you* intend to sell her."

"Nope." Relieved that Kaylee's horse had been found, Colt grinned. "Where did you find her?"

"Down in the Texas panhandle. When the guy at the sale barn Kaylee had used to sell the Lazy S livestock told us the buyer was from down that way, Brant got in touch with his old rodeo buddy Cooper Adams." Morgan chuckled. "Two hours later we knew who owned her, and how much it would take to buy her."

"I've always liked Coop," Colt said, grinning. "How soon can I go down to pick her up?"

"You don't have to," Morgan answered. Colt

could hear the smile in his brother's voice. "Cooper's sister, Jenna, and her husband, Flint, are heading up to Denver for a horse show anyway. They're going to load the mare in their horse trailer and bring her with them. Brant and I are going to drive down Monday morning to get her."

Colt couldn't have asked for more. "I owe you and Brant one."

"We were glad to help you find the mare," Morgan said seriously. "We knew Mitch gave it to Kaylee and how much the horse meant to her."

"Thanks, Morgan."

After they said goodbye, Colt walked out of the study and, taking the stairs two at a time, strode purposefully down the hall to Amber's room. He couldn't wait to let Kaylee know about her horse.

"Kaylee, I've got something to tell you," he said, entering his daughter's dimly lit bedroom.

He found Kaylee sitting in the rocking chair on the far side of the room, slowly rocking Amber. She placed her index finger to her lips to silence him. "She just went to sleep," she whispered.

"Sorry," he mouthed, walking over to stand next to them.

As he watched Kaylee cuddle Amber to her, his chest tightened and he forgot all about the reason he'd sought her out. If he lived to be as old as Methuselah he didn't think he'd ever see a more beautiful sight.

When Kaylee moved to get up from the chair, Colt reached out to take his sleeping daughter from her. His hand brushed Kaylee's breast as he lifted Amber into his arms and he barely managed to suppress a groan.

"I told you this afternoon not to lift anything heavier than the three-pound weight," Kaylee whispered hotly.

He chuckled. "And I told you I could lift that much with my little finger," he said just as quietly.

He wasn't going to tell her about the little twinge he'd felt in his shoulder. It wasn't anything significant and he'd much rather savor the moment of helping Kaylee put their little girl to bed.

Laying Amber down, he smiled as Kaylee covered her with a colorful quilt. "Thank you, honey."

Straightening, she frowned. "What for?"

Colt took her into his arms. "For giving me the most precious gift a woman can give a man—his child."

Kaylee rested her head against his chest and wrapped her arms around his waist as they both stared down at their sleeping daughter. "I should be thanking you," she said softly. "Amber is the best thing that's ever happened to me. From the moment I suspected I was pregnant with her, I was thrilled."

Her quiet statement seemed to rob him of breath. All things considered, most women would have been fit to be tied by an unexpected pregnancy. But

Kaylee had been happy about him making her pregnant?

"Why, Kaylee?" he asked, needing to know. "Why were you happy at the prospect of having a baby?"

She leaned back to stare up at him. Uncertainty clouded her violet gaze a moment before she took a deep breath and whispered, "Because I knew the baby was a part of you."

Colt's heart stalled, then took off at a dead run. Kaylee had welcomed his child, loved and nurtured her, even before she'd known for sure that Amber was growing in her belly.

His knees threatened to buckle and he had a hard time expressing how much her admission meant to him. Groaning, he simply lowered his mouth to hers, letting her know without words what he was feeling.

At the first touch of Kaylee's sweet lips to his, Colt's temperature shot skyward and a lazy warmth began to gather in the pit of his stomach. But when he deepened the kiss, every nerve in his body sparked to life and a shimmering heat began to race through his veins.

Bringing his hand up along her side, he gently cupped her breast and was rewarded by her soft moan vibrating against his mouth. The sound sent his pulse into overdrive and his good intentions right out the window.

He'd told her they would allow their feelings to

build before they took the next step in their relationship. But it had been three long years since he'd
made love to her, and the need to once again make
Kaylee his tightened his body to an almost painful
state and clouded his mind.

Taking things slowly was no longer an option for
them. As she melted against him, Colt wasn't sure
that it had ever been. He wanted Kaylee with a need
that staggered him and he sensed that the same hunger that had seized him, had her in its grips, as well.

When he broke the kiss and lifted his head, he
glanced at their daughter, then at the woman in his
arms. "I want to make love with you, Kaylee. I want
to be buried so deeply inside of you that we both
lose sight of where I end and you begin." He
brushed a lock of auburn hair from her satiny cheek.
"Is that what you want?"

Indecision crossed her lovely features, and just
when he thought she was going to tell him she
wasn't ready to take that step, she closed her eyes
and nodded. "I've never wanted anything more in
my life than to be loved by you, Colt."

Eight

Kaylee watched Colt's vivid blue gaze darken. Then, releasing her, he stepped back to take her by the hand. "Let's go to my room, honey."

Her stomach fluttered as if a thousand tiny butterflies had been unleashed inside of her and her knees felt like rubber as she let Colt lead her out of Amber's room and down the hall. A tiny part of her was frightened that she could very easily be making the biggest mistake of her life, that she might be setting herself up for more of the same shattering disappointment she'd experienced three years ago. But her heart told her that she'd never really had a choice in the matter. From the moment she'd first laid eyes on Colt Wakefield fourteen years ago, she'd loved him.

When they entered his bedroom, he walked over to the bedside table and switched on the lamp, then turned to face her. "Kaylee, I don't want you feeling pressured." He gently cupped her cheeks with his hands. "If you're not ready for this, I want you to tell me now. I don't ever want you to regret making love with me."

She took a deep breath as she gazed into his eyes and told him what she knew in her heart to be true. "I won't regret making love with you, Colt."

He stared at her for endless seconds, then pulled her to him. She felt a shudder run through his body at the same moment a groan rumbled up from deep in his chest. "You can't imagine how much that means to me, honey."

Before she could respond he covered her mouth with his and Kaylee felt as if the butterflies in her stomach had gone absolutely berserk. But when he traced her lips with his tongue, then entered her mouth to stroke her with a rhythm that left her breathless, the fluttering sensation spread to every cell of her being.

Tasting Colt's passion, feeling his strong arousal pressed to her soft lower belly, made her knees wobble and she found that she had to cling to him to keep from melting into a puddle at his feet. She'd always thought his kiss was devastating, but this time she could tell that he held nothing back, and she felt branded by the extent of his hunger.

When he raised his head, his breathing was labored. "I'm going to try to take this slow. But I've never wanted a woman as much as I want you."

"I want you, too," she said, feeling just as breathless.

"Are you on the pill or the patch, honey?"

Kaylee cheeks grew warm. Discussing something so intimate was slightly embarrassing. But not addressing the issue a few years ago was the very reason she was at the Lonetree now.

"I, um, haven't had to worry about birth control," she said, shaking her head.

He sucked in a sharp breath. "Kaylee, I know I have no right to ask, but—"

"There hasn't been anyone else since that night with you," she said quietly.

Colt's heart slammed against his ribs and he felt as if he might never breathe again. Kaylee had been a virgin three years ago, and the knowledge that he'd been the only man she'd ever made love with sent his blood pressure into stroke range.

He closed his eyes, took a deep breath, then opened them to gaze down at her. "I promise this time you don't have to worry, honey." Giving her a quick kiss, he bent to remove her tennis shoes and his boots, then straightened to tug her T-shirt from the waistband of her jeans. He slid his hands beneath the hem to lift the garment up and over her arms. "I'll take care of protecting you."

With a smile that sent a surge of heat straight to the region south of his belt buckle, she began to unfasten the snaps on his chambray shirt. When she peeled it back and placed her warm palms on his heated skin, Colt felt as if a slow-burning fuse had been ignited deep inside him.

"Did anyone ever tell you what a gorgeous body you have, cowboy?" she asked, running her hands over the muscles of his chest and abdomen.

"Honey, I've been called a lot of things, but I don't ever remember the word 'gorgeous' being used to describe me," he said, chuckling. He started to tell her that she was the one who was beautiful, but she lightly grazed his flat nipples with the tips of her fingernails and a strangled groan came out instead.

Her busy little hands stilled. "Do you want me to stop?"

Unable to get his vocal cords to work, he shook his head and watched as she continued to trace the now puckered flesh.

When they'd made love before, it had been an urgent coupling—a desperate attempt to escape the pain of losing Mitch. But this time was different. This time they were exploring, learning what was pleasing and what brought the most pleasure.

No longer willing or able to keep from touching her, Colt reached behind Kaylee to unhook her plain white bra, then slid the straps from her shoulders to toss it on top of her shirt. His hands shook slightly as he cupped her firm breasts in his calloused palms, then chafed the tight tips with the pads of his thumbs.

A soft moan escaped her lips. "Mmm."

"Feel good?" he asked as he continued to tease her.

"Y-yes."

He leaned down to kiss one perfect coral bud, then took it into his mouth to taste her sweetness. When she swayed, he wrapped an arm around her waist to support her while he turned his attention to her other nipple.

Raising his head, he kissed her forehead, her eyes and the tip of her nose. "So sweet. So perfect."

She moved to ease his shirt from his shoulders. "I think you're overdressed, don't you, cowboy?"

"Not for long," he said, reaching for his belt buckle.

To his delight, she shook her head and shooed his hands away. "Let me take care of that for you."

"The last time you unfastened my belt, you were mad at me," he said, remembering the night they spent in the motel on the way to the Lonetree.

"You deserved that. You were running the risk of reinjuring your collarbone by doing too much, too soon," she said, making short work of freeing the leather strap from the buckle.

''But you're not upset with me now?'' he asked, grinning.

She shook her head and started to release the button at his waistband. ''At the moment, anger is the last thing I'm feeling.''

Her fingers brushed his lower belly and he felt as if a surge of heat shot straight to his groin. Taking a deep breath, he reached for the belt encircling her small waist. Making quick work of unbuckling it, he released the button at the top of her jeans, unzipped them, then slid them and her sensible white cotton panties down her slender legs.

When she stepped out of them, her gaze met his and the look in her violet eyes damn near brought him to his knees as she reached for the metal tab at the top of his fly. He held his breath as she eased the zipper down over his arousal straining insistently at the fabric of his boxer briefs. But when she placed her hands just inside the elastic band, and shoved them and his jeans down his legs, Colt felt as if he just might go into total meltdown.

Suddenly looking uncertain, she stepped back. Noticing the direction of her gaze, he gave her a reassuring smile before pulling her to him. But the contrast of her soft femininity against his hard male flesh, the feel of her pebbled nipples pressing into his skin, hastened the sizzling fuse burning inside him and he had to take several deep breaths to hang on to his rapidly slipping control.

"You feel so damned good," he said through clenched teeth.

"Colt—"

Gazing at her pretty face, he noticed the blush of passion on her porcelain cheeks, and he could tell she was feeling the same burning need that he was. "Do you trust me, Kaylee?"

"Yes."

He smiled. "It's going to be okay."

"I-it's been so long, Colt."

"I know, honey. But I promise this time there won't be any discomfort." He kissed her forehead. "I'm going to make sure that it's nothing but pure pleasure for you."

He slid his hands down her back to cup her delightful bottom and pulled her to him. The feel of his arousal nestled against her soft warmth had him gritting his teeth and praying for the strength to go slow.

"Don't ever doubt that I'm attracted to you, Kaylee," he finally managed to say. "Or that I want you."

He felt her tremble, then, without a word, she took his hand in hers and led him over to the side of his king-size bed. Pulling back the covers, she laid down, then smiled at him.

"I'll be right back, honey," he said, walking into the adjoining bathroom.

When he returned, he tucked a foil packet beneath his pillow and stretched out beside her on the bed.

Taking her into his arms, he kissed her until they were both gasping for breath.

''I want you to tell me what feels good,'' he said, sliding his hand along her side.

Kaylee's skin tingled from Colt's touch and heat flowed through her veins, threading its way to the very core of her being. A coil of need began to form in the pit of her stomach as his lips nibbled a path from the pulse fluttering at the base of her throat over her collarbone and down the slope of her breast. He took the tight tip into his mouth, then flicked it with his tongue, causing her heart to skip a beat and her breathing to become shallow.

Tangling her hands in his thick raven hair, she held him to her as wave after wave of pleasure swept over her and the coil in her belly tightened. The first time they'd made love, it had been hurried and reckless as they both tried to forget their grief. But this time they were taking their time as they explored each other and the compelling magnetism pulling them together.

When Colt raised his head to gaze down at her, the look in his eyes stole her breath. ''Honey, I want you so damned much I ache from it.''

He lowered his head to kiss her as he slid his hand down to her hip. The feel of his firm lips on hers, his calloused palm on her skin, and the insistence of his arousal pressed to her thigh, caused Kaylee to bite her lower lip in an effort to stifle the moan threatening to escape. But when he moved his hand to the apex of her thighs, she shivered with a need like nothing she'd ever before experienced. His fingers searched for and found her pleasure point and she couldn't hold in the sound of her passion any longer.

"What do you want, Kaylee?" he whispered close to her ear.

"I want...you, Colt," she said, barely recognizing the throaty voice as her own. Wanting to touch him as he touched her, she reached down to stroke him with infinite care. "Only you."

She felt a shudder run through his big body a moment before he groaned and buried his head in the curve of her neck. He caught her hand in his and brought it to his chest.

"Honey, if you keep that up I'm not going to make it past the eight-second whistle."

"Then make love to me, Colt," she said, wanting him more than she'd ever dreamed possible.

He kissed her, then reached under his pillow. Once he had the condom in place, he took her in his arms and nudged her knees apart.

Looking up into eyes so blue she felt as if she might drown in their depths, Kaylee was lost. His smoldering gaze held her captive as without a word, he gathered her close and slowly, gently, pressed forward to make their bodies one. She tensed and held her breath at the exquisite stretching.

"Just relax, honey," he said when he'd completely filled her.

She felt his body quiver as he fought for control. A muscle jerked along his lean jaw and she could tell what his restraint was costing him.

Touching his cheeks with trembling fingers, she pulled his handsome face down to kiss his firm, warm lips. "Colt, I need—"

He opened his eyes and gave her a look that caused her pulse to race. "Kaylee, I want to make this last, but it's been so long and you feel so damn good."

She felt the same way. But unable to find the words to express what she needed, she simply wrapped her legs around his narrow hips as she tried to get closer.

"Honey, I think you're going to kill me," he said, groaning.

He threaded his fingers in her hair and kissed her passionately as he pulled back then moved forward. Her body responded with an answering motion and together they found the rhythm that would take them to a place only lovers go.

Her heart swelled with emotion as he cradled her in his arms and her world was reduced to just the two of them—one man, one woman coming together in the age-old dance of love. Surrounded by Colt, being filled by him, quickly had Kaylee climbing toward the peak, reaching for the unknown. Heat flowed through her and she moaned from the tightening of the coil deep inside her.

Apparently sensing her readiness, Colt quickened

the pace. "Let it happen, Kaylee. I'm right here with you, honey."

Suddenly feeling as if stars burst within her soul, she spun out of control, her universe reduced to the man holding her body to his. Light danced behind her closed eyes and pleasure shimmered over every cell in her being as with one final thrust Colt joined her and together they soared on the current of perfect fulfillment.

Drifting back to reality, love so pure it brought tears to her eyes filled her and she held him close, reluctant for the moment to end. She wasn't sure where their relationship was headed, or if they had a future together. But the one thing that would never change, no matter what happened between them was the depth of her love for him.

At the age of ten she'd loved him with a child's innocent adoration. But at twenty-four, she loved him with a woman's passionate heart. And she knew beyond a shadow of doubt that she always would.

"We have one more stop to make before we start back home," Annie said.

Grinning, Samantha nodded. "We always save the best for last."

As they all walked out of the restaurant where they'd had lunch, Kaylee watched the two women exchange a knowing smile. She'd seen that look before. It was the same amused expression they'd worn the night they baby-sat Amber.

''What's going on?'' She looked from one woman to the other. ''Is there something I should know about?''

''It's nothing really,'' Samantha said, shaking her head. ''Annie and I just need to buy some new, um, under things.''

Kaylee laughed. ''Since when is buying underwear special?''

''It's where we shop that makes the difference,'' Annie and Samantha said in unison.

Kaylee frowned. ''Where do you—'' She stopped suddenly. ''Oh, dear heavens! You two shop at the—''

''Sleek and Sassy Lady Lingerie Boutique,'' Annie said, laughing.

Samantha suddenly looked uncertain. ''Kaylee, I, uh, that is, we don't know what your relationship is with Colt, and it's none of our business. If you'd rather not go shopping for lingerie, we'll understand.''

''Absolutely,'' Annie said, nodding.

Kaylee nibbled on her lower lip. She remembered the expressions on Brant's and Morgan's faces when the shopping trip was mentioned. The two men hadn't been able to hide their anticipation for what their wives might bring home.

''I've never worn anything but plain white cotton,'' she said, thinking out loud. Her cheeks heated as she tried to decide how to ask a question that might be a little too personal. ''I don't mean to be nosy, but do your husbands really like what you buy?''

Looking relieved that Kaylee hadn't been offended, both women laughed.

''There are four things that the Wakefield men have in common,'' Annie said. ''Black hair, blue eyes, their love of the Lonetree Ranch, and…they have a deep appreciation for the Sleek and Sassy Lady Lingerie Boutique.''

''We're betting Colt is no different,'' Samantha added, grinning.

''I…oh, heavens,'' Kaylee stammered, blushing.

Did she really have the nerve to buy sexy underwear? Would Colt like seeing her in provocative undies? Something told her that he would be just as enthusiastic about it as his older brothers.

''Maybe this was a bad idea,'' Samantha said, frowning.

Annie shook her head. ''Forget we mentioned it, Kaylee.''

Kaylee took a deep breath, then smiled at her two friends. ''Actually, I think…'' She giggled nervously. ''…I'd like to see if Colt has the same appreciation for lingerie that his brothers have.''

Samantha laughed. ''Then let's go see what we can find that will knock that man's socks off.''

An hour later Kaylee walked out of the mall carrying several bags with the Sleek and Sassy Lady logo on them. Colt had given her his credit card, but she'd used her own money for the lingerie. She wasn't about to use his card for her underwear. Some things were highly personal and sexy undies were one of them.

"I really like that white lace teddy you bought," Annie said, juggling her own bags as she dug for the keys to her SUV. "As soon as I have the baby I think I'll go back and buy one in royal blue."

"I like that emerald camisole and matching thong," Samantha added. "With your peaches-and-cream complexion and auburn hair, it's really going to look nice, Kaylee."

"I just hope I have the nerve to wear this stuff," Kaylee said, laughing. "It's all so different from my white cotton—"

"Granny panties," Samantha and Annie said at the same time.

"Well, I wasn't going to call them that," Kaylee said, laughing. "But I'd say that's a pretty accurate description."

"When are you going to spring your new look on Colt?" Samantha asked as they stored the packages in the back of Annie's Explorer.

"I'm not sure, but it'll have to be soon." Kaylee felt a pang of sadness knife through her. "I'm due back at my job soon."

"You're not staying?" Samantha asked, clearly shocked. "But I thought—"

Kaylee shrugged one shoulder. She and Colt hadn't discussed what would happen when it was time for her to return to Oklahoma. "It's complicated."

"Are you going to the PBR finals with Colt?" Annie asked.

"I...can't." Kaylee shook her head and took a deep, steadying breath. "Not after what happened to Mitch."

Annie reached out to hug her. "I hope you're able to work it out between you two."

"I do, too," Samantha said, hugging Kaylee when Annie released her. "We want you to stay on at the Lonetree."

Kaylee fought her threatening tears as they got into the SUV and drove from the mall parking lot onto the highway. She wanted nothing more than for her, Colt and Amber to be a family and to live on the Lonetree Ranch together.

But Colt was a bull rider, and although she couldn't bear the thought of something happening to him, she wouldn't ask him to give that up. It would be like asking him to give up who he was. And that was something she just couldn't do.

Nine

Colt waited impatiently while Kaylee went upstairs to put away some laundry she'd done as soon as she'd returned from shopping with Annie and Samantha. "This is one surprise I think your mommy's going to like," he told Amber as he helped her into her little jean jacket.

He frowned as he glanced toward the stairs. What could be taking Kaylee so long? She'd told him she'd be right back, but that had been fifteen minutes ago.

When she finally walked across the loft area, then started down the stairs, she was smiling. "You both look quite smug. Were you waiting on me for a reason?"

Nodding, Colt caught her around the waist and pulled her to him. "We've missed you something awful," he said, giving her a quick kiss.

"I missed you, too." She smiled. "What did you two do while I was gone, watch television the whole time?"

He shook his head. "Nope. We visited with Morgan and Brant for a while this morning—"

"But I thought they were supposed to be watching the boys," Kaylee said, frowning.

"They had Bettylou Milford baby-sit while they brought...er, ran an errand for me." He shrugged nonchalantly in an effort to dismiss the importance of their visit.

"Doggie," Amber said, grinning.

"Did you see a doggie?" Kaylee asked, smiling at their daughter.

"Yes," Amber said, shaking her head negatively.

Colt was thankful Kaylee had no idea that Amber was referring to the horse his brothers had brought over earlier. To keep her from asking questions, he hurried on. "After Brant and Morgan left, Amber and I made peanut butter and jelly sandwiches and watched the veggie show."

"Mato," Amber said, holding out her arms for him to pick her up.

Colt swung her up to sit on his right forearm. Holding Kaylee and his daughter, he was once again struck by the feeling that his life was more complete than it had ever been.

"Why does Amber have her jacket on?" Kaylee asked suddenly. "Were you two going somewhere?"

"Yep." He couldn't stop his ear-to-ear grin. "And we're taking you with us."

Kaylee laughed. "Where are we going?"

Colt winked at Amber as he put her down then took her little hand in his. "Oh, just out to the barn."

"Born," Amber said, giggling. "Doggie."

Reaching for Kaylee's hand, he led them out the door and down the porch steps. "I want you to close your eyes, Kaylee."

"Another surprise?" she asked, raising one perfect eyebrow.

"Yes. But this time, I promise you're going to like it."

She gave him a smile that made him weak in the knees. "You're that sure, huh?"

"Yep." He rocked back on his heels. "Now, close your eyes." He waited until she'd done as he'd requested, then started leading her toward the barn. "Don't open them until I tell you to."

"This isn't something that's going to jump out at me, is it?" she asked, her tone cautious.

"Nope." When they entered the barn, he led her and Amber over to the two saddled horses, standing tied to the outside of a stall. "Okay, honey, you can open your eyes."

He couldn't stop grinning as he watched Kaylee apprehensively open one eye, then the other.

She blinked as if she couldn't quite believe what she was seeing. "Oh my God, Colt!" She covered her mouth with both hands, then turned to stare at him, her eyes wide. "Where did you get…I mean how did you find…" Her voice trailed off as her eyes filled with tears. Throwing her arms around his neck, she kissed his cheek. "I can't believe you found my horse."

He put his arm around her waist and held her to him. "I take it you like the surprise?"

"Oh, Colt, thank you for finding her," Kaylee said, kissing him again before she pulled away to approach the buckskin.

"Doggie," Amber said, pointing to the horses.

Picking Amber up, Colt laughed as he untied the buckskin mare and the bay gelding, then handed the mare's reins to Kaylee. "No, pixie. These are horses, and when you get old enough, Daddy's going to get you one, too."

"I can't wait to ride my horse again," Kaylee said, patting the mare's neck as they led the two animals out of the barn. When she turned and kissed him again, he decided it would have been worth twice what he'd had to pay for the mare just to see Kaylee this happy.

"Go ahead and mount up," he said, unable to stop grinning. "Amber and I are right behind you."

Lifting his daughter onto the back of the gelding, he put his boot in the stirrup and swung up onto the saddle. Settling Amber on his lap, he wrapped his arm around her little body, then flicked the reins. The bay took off at a slow walk, sending Amber into a fit of giggles.

"You like riding with Mommy and Daddy?" Colt ask as he and Kaylee rode out of the yard and into the pasture to the west of the barn.

"No," Amber said, nodding her head.

"Colt, would you mind if I—"

"Go right ahead, honey," he said, knowing that Kaylee wanted to put the mare through her paces.

Kaylee immediately nudged the mare into a canter, then, giving the horse her head, raced across the open meadow toward the slow-moving stream on the other side of the valley. She was a very accomplished horsewoman and it was clear she was having the time of her life. And he was having the time of his life watching her.

Her long auburn hair was in attractive disarray and her cheeks were pink from the wind in her face. But it was her obvious happiness that tightened his chest with emotion. She was happier than he'd seen her since before Mitch died.

Colt smiled. He could spend an entire lifetime and never get tired of making Kaylee happy.

Sucking in a sharp breath, he pulled the bay to a halt. Had he fallen in love with Kaylee?

His heart pounded against his ribs. He'd always liked her and when he'd realized that she'd grown into a beautiful woman, he'd desired her. But love?

He'd known for years that she'd had a crush on him, and although he'd been extremely attracted to her, he'd always put a clamp on his feelings. That is, until that night three years ago.

Thinking about that night, he'd convinced himself that he'd taken off the next morning because of feeling guilty and ashamed for taking advantage of her. But had he really been running from himself? Had he been in love with her then?

As he continued to stare at Kaylee riding the mare, a slow grin spread across his face. Hell, truth to tell he'd always loved her. He'd just been too damned blind to see it.

"Amber, your daddy's been a fool," he said, kissing the top of her little head. "But now that he's come to his senses, he's going to make up for lost time with your mommy."

Amber pointed to Kaylee, riding toward them. "Mommy, doggie."

Feeling younger and happier than he had in a long time, Colt laughed out loud. "One of these days I'll get you a horse and a dog, too, little pixie. But right now, Daddy's got to find the perfect time to tell your mommy what an idiot he's been and how he'd like to spend the rest of his life telling her how much he loves her.''

''I can't believe how out of shape I am,'' Kaylee muttered as she straightened the kitchen.

It seemed as if every muscle from her waist down had decided to rebel. But as much as she hurt, it had felt absolutely wonderful to be riding her mare again. She hadn't realized how much she'd missed feeling the wind in her hair and the graceful power of a horse moving beneath her.

Tears filled her eyes when she thought of how considerate Colt's gesture had been. He'd known how much the horse meant to her. It had been the last thing Mitch had given her before his death and it had broken her heart to have to sell the animal. But now that Colt owned the mare, maybe she'd get to ride the horse occasionally, whenever she brought Amber to the Lonetree for a visit.

Thoughts of going back home caused her chest to tighten. She hadn't wanted to come to the Lonetree because she'd feared falling in love with Colt again. She almost laughed out loud. The truth of the matter was, she'd never stopped loving him.

But even if, by some miracle, he'd fallen head over heels in love with her, Kaylee didn't see them having a future together. Not as long as he continued to ride bulls. Just the thought of him being hurt or…

A chill ran through her. She couldn't bring herself to think about the worst that could happen.

Two strong arms suddenly wrapped around her from behind and pulled her back against a wide chest. "What are you thinking about, honey?"

She closed her eyes to block out the disturbing thought before she turned in the circle of Colt's arms to smile up at him. "I'm thinking about how much I appreciate you finding my horse, and how wonderful it was to be riding her again." She winced when her calf muscle cramped. "Even if my legs don't agree."

His deep blue gaze held her captive. "Pretty sore, huh?"

Groaning, she nodded. "I'm discovering muscles I forgot I had."

"Why don't you go upstairs and soak in the Jacuzzi?" he asked, brushing his lips lightly over hers.

Time in a whirlpool sounded like heaven to Kaylee, but she still had things to do. "I wish I could. But I need to get Amber ready for bed."

"Why don't you relax this evening and let me get her settled down for the night?" he asked, nuzzling the column of her neck.

Shivers of excitement coursed through her from the feel of his warm breath and lips moving over her sensitive skin. "D-do you think you can handle her bath?" she asked, trying to form a coherent answer. She was tempted by the idea of soaking some of the soreness from her aching muscles, but Colt had never dealt with a two-year-old at bath time. "There are times when giving her a bath can be a real trial."

"Hey, I ride bulls for a living." He chuckled. "How hard can it be to get one little girl into bed for the night?"

"It might prove more difficult than you think," Kaylee said, ignoring his reference to his job. She didn't want to think about that now. He was holding her and that was all that mattered.

"Up, Daddy."

Colt bent to pick up Amber. "Why don't we get her ready for bed together?" Grinning, he added, "Then I can help you with your bath."

Kaylee's cheeks heated and her insides felt as if they'd turned to warm pudding at his suggestion. "We'll see."

"Hey, no fair, pixie," Colt said, looking down at the wet spot spreading across his shirt.

"Daddy wet," Amber said happily. She gave him a grin that melted his heart, then slapped the top of her bathwater again with her hand.

This time the splash covered Colt's face. "Kaylee!"

"Problems?"

He turned to see her causally leaning one shoulder against the door frame, a big smile on her pretty face. "Why didn't you tell me our daughter likes water sports?" he asked, reaching for the fluffy towel hanging on a rack beside the tub.

"And miss the fun of watching Amber teach her daddy what bath time is like with a two-year-old?" Grinning, she shook her head. "I don't think so, cowboy."

He wiped the water dripping off his face. "Is it always like this?"

"Oh, sometimes it's even worse," Kaylee said, laughing.

He gazed down at his happy daughter. "You wouldn't splash me more than you already have, would you?"

As if in answer, Amber kicked both legs and slapped the water with both hands, proving just how much worse giving her a bath could get.

"Okay. Okay. I get the idea," he said, laughing.

By the time Colt lifted his happy little girl from the bathtub and handed her to Kaylee, there wasn't a dry thread on him from his collar to his belt. "I'm soaked to the bone."

"I'll take pity on you and rock her to sleep," Kaylee said, toweling Amber dry, then pulling a pink nightgown over her little head. "Why don't you go find a dry shirt to put on?"

"Sounds good to me." He got to his feet and kissed Amber. "'Night, little pixie." Walking to the bathroom door, he turned back to grin at Kaylee. "I think from now on, I'll let you give her a bath and I'll do the rocking.''

As he walked down the hall to his room, her laughter sounded like music to his ears. She was having a grand old time at his expense. And he loved every minute of it.

By the time he entered his room, Colt had his shirt unsnapped. It was drenched and, entering the master bath to drape it over the towel rack, he eyed the oversize Jacuzzi. What was the use of having a bathtub two people could fit into if he didn't share?

Without hesitation, he turned on the polished gold faucet, set the dimmer switch on the lights to a muted setting, then sat on the side of the tub to pull off his boots. Shucking his jeans, socks and boxer briefs, he turned on the jets, climbed into the water and lounged against the back.

A few minutes later, he smiled when he heard Kaylee softly call his name as she entered his bedroom. ''Colt, where are you?''

''In here, honey.''

When Kaylee walked into the bathroom, he motioned for her to join him. ''I decided to get the water ready for you.''

''I thought I was the one getting the use of the Jacuzzi this evening,'' she said, giving him a smile that made him feel as if the water temperature had risen by about ten degrees.

''I'm a man of my word, honey,'' he said, grinning. "I told you I'd help you with your bath, and that's just what I intend to do."

He watched her nervously nibble at her lower lip for a moment before she took a deep breath and reached to pull her T-shirt from the waistband of her jeans. "Have Morgan or Brant ever mentioned Samantha and Annie's shopping trips?"

"No, but they sure seem to like when the women mention a trip to the mall." Frowning, he shook his head. "But I don't want to talk about—"

He stopped short and sat up straight when Kaylee pulled her purple shirt over her head and tossed it aside. Until now, when he'd taken her clothes off of her, she'd worn a plain white bra with no frills. But tonight she was wearing the skimpiest scrap of black lace and satin he'd ever seen.

"Is that—" he had to stop to clear the rust from his throat "—something you bought today?"

She nodded. "Do you like it?"

"Hell, yes."

He started to tell her that he'd like it better off of her, but her smile promised that the show wasn't over yet. Settling back against the tub, he looked forward to what she had planned next. To his delight, he didn't have long to wait.

Watching her unbutton the top of her jeans, then slowly slide the zipper down was heaven and hell rolled into one for him. His eyes widened and he knew for certain he'd never seen anything quite as provocative as the look she gave him when she pushed the denim down her slender legs. But catching sight of the triangle of lace and satin barely covering her feminine secrets, Colt wasn't sure his eyes weren't going to pop right out of his head. Made to match her bra, the set was enough to bury a man with any kind of heart problems.

"H-honey, where did you get those?" he finally managed to ask.

"The Sleek and Sassy Lady Lingerie Boutique."

"I think that's my favorite store," he said, meaning it.

"Annie and Samantha said Brant and Morgan have a deep appreciation for the items the store carries," she said, making a slow turn for him to get the full effect of what she was wearing.

"Oh, yeah. I'm appreciating the hell out of it right now." He swallowed hard when he realized the little triangle showed more of her delightful bottom than it hid. "Damn, Kaylee, that little patch of satin could be considered a lethal weapon."

She smiled. "Now do you understand why your brothers like for their wives to visit the mall?"

Feeling as if his blood pressure was reaching the danger zone, he nodded.

As he watched, she touched the clasp between her breasts. "I have several new sets of matching under things—" she unfastened the closure, then slipped the thin straps down her arms and tossed the miniscule scrap on top of her shirt "—in various colors and styles."

If he could have found his voice, he would have told her that he was looking forward to seeing her model each set. Unfortunately he couldn't seem to get his vocal cords to work. But when she hooked her thumbs in the waistband of the panties and slowly pulled them down, a groan rumbled up from deep in his chest and his heart damn near thumped a hole right through his rib cage.

Colt closed his eyes and tried to drag some much needed air into his lungs. He was so turned on that if he didn't slow down, he was going to blow a gasket right then and there.

"Those stores should get some kind of special award for being a man's best friend," he said, breathing deeply in an effort to hang on to his control.

When he felt Kaylee step into the tub, he opened his eyes and helped her to sit between his legs. Wrapping his arms around her, he pulled her back to lie against him. He gritted his teeth at the feel of her smooth skin pressed to his chest, her bottom nestled against the part of him that was changing so rapidly it made him light-headed.

She sighed. "The Sleek and Sassy Lady Lingerie Boutique chain might be a man's best friend, but this whirlpool is mine."

He kissed the side of her head as he put his hands

on her thighs and massaged her tight muscles. ''Is that feeling a little better, honey?'' he asked when he felt her begin to relax.

''Mmm.''

The water made her smooth skin slippery and he easily slid his hands up her thighs and over her abdomen to cup her full breasts. His body throbbed from the feel of her pressed against the most vulnerable part of him. The tightening of her nipples as he teased them only increased his arousal.

''Kaylee?''

When she turned her head to look up at him, he captured her mouth with his and, tracing her lips with his tongue, he slipped it inside to taste the sweetness that was uniquely Kaylee. He loved holding her, kissing her. Hell, he just plain loved everything about her. And he fully intended to tell her so when he had enough of his wits about him to form words.

But at the moment he was lost to anything but the feel of her filling his hands, the taste of her passion and the sound of her labored breathing. The knowledge that she wanted him as much as he wanted her fueled the fire building within him.

Leisurely sliding one hand down her wet body to the apex of her thighs, he parted her to gently stroke the tiny nub nestled within. Her moan of pleasure vibrating against his lips heightened his own excitement, and Colt felt blood surge through his veins, tightening his body, urging him to once again make her his.

Breaking the kiss, he whispered, "Turn around, Kaylee. I want to love you."

"But—"

He chuckled. "Trust me, honey. It can be done."

To his satisfaction, she didn't even hesitate as she maneuvered herself around to face him. He scooted forward, then helped her drape her legs over his thighs.

"See, it's not as difficult as you thought," he said, pressing a kiss to her perfect lips, her chin and her collarbone.

When he continued to nibble his way down the slope of her breast, Colt felt a tremor run through her a moment before she circled his neck with her arms and curled her legs around his hips. Her head fell back to give him better access. Taking advantage of the position, he took her nipple in his mouth to suck her gently.

"Colt, I…need—"

Lifting his head, he watched her slowly open her eyes. The passion and love he saw in the violet depths robbed him of breath.

Without a word, Colt lowered his mouth to hers as he lifted her to him and in one smooth motion joined their bodies. The feel of Kaylee surrounding him, the sound of her soft sigh and the taste of desire on her sweet lips blocked out all reason and left him with nothing but the ability to complete the act of loving her.

He held her hips and guided her in a rocking motion that quickly had him gritting his teeth against the urgent need to race for the peak. His body throbbed and his heart pounded, but he refused to give in to his own satisfaction before he was assured he'd helped Kaylee find hers.

When he felt her inner feminine muscles tighten around him, signaling that she was close to finding her completion, he reached between them to stroke her. The moment his finger touched her, she went completely still, then, whispering his name, he felt her body quiver around him as she was released from the exquisite tension inside her.

Only then did he give in to the storm raging inside him and surrender the tight hold he had on his control. Surging into her one final time, he groaned as he emptied his essence deep within her warm depths.

As the whirlpool jets worked their magic and lulled them back to the realm of reality, he held Kaylee close. He'd done the unthinkable. He'd failed to protect her. Much the way he'd done three years ago, he'd let his need to brand her as his override his good sense.

But as he caressed her soft body, it came as no small surprise that he wasn't sorry. Nothing would please him more than to create another child with

Kaylee, of seeing her belly grow round as his baby grew inside her.

Unfortunately he wasn't sure how she felt about giving Amber a little brother or sister. Nor had they discussed their future together.

He was sure she loved him and there wasn't a doubt in his mind that he loved her. But knowing how he made his living, would she be willing to marry him?

"Kaylee?"

"Mmm."

"Do you have any idea how much I love you?"

He heard her soft intake of breath a moment before she leaned back to gaze up at him. "Y-you love me?"

Unable to stop grinning, Colt nodded. "I always have. I was just too big of a fool to admit it."

Tears filled her pretty violet eyes. "Oh, Colt. I've loved you from the first minute I set eyes on you."

His heart soared. Everything was going to be all right. They'd work something out. They had to. There was no way he was going to take a chance on screwing this up a second time.

Kissing her creamy shoulder, he smiled. "Let's get out of the tub, honey. We need to talk."

Ten

"Kaylee, I want you and Amber to go with me to the PBR finals in Vegas."

Sitting in the middle of Colt's bed, Kaylee gazed into his vivid blue eyes and fought the urge to tell him that she would go with him. Pulling her chenille robe more tightly around her, she shivered violently. She loved him more than life itself, but he was asking something of her that she just couldn't do.

"Colt, I love you. I'll always love you." She shook her head. "But I can't watch you ride bulls."

He took her hands in his. "Honey, I know you're afraid something might happen to me. But you've always known what I did for a living and you accepted it."

"T-that was before." She pulled away from him and got out of bed before his touch and the beseeching expression on his handsome face caused her to weaken.

"Honey, I'm close to winning the championship," Colt argued. "I can't quit now."

Pacing the length of his room, she tried to explain how she felt. "Colt, I would never ask you to stop being a bull rider. It's a part of you—it's who you are." Feeling as if she might choke on the emotions welling up inside of her, she stopped to catch her breath. "But I can't bear the thought of watching you being taken out of an arena like Mitch was that night in Houston."

"Kaylee, you know I'm always careful. I keep myself in good shape and—"

"Mitch was in as good a shape as any of the riders and he was always careful," she said, impatiently wiping at a tear running down her cheek. "And look what happened to him."

"But—"

She shook her head. "Colt, I couldn't survive standing in another hospital waiting room while some doctor tells me there's nothing he could do to save your life." Chills racked her body and she couldn't stop shaking. "I just can't…do that again," she whispered.

He got out of bed and, walking over to her, wrapped her in his strong arms. "Kaylee, life doesn't come with any kind of guarantee. Something could happen to me no matter what I do for a living.''

''I...know that,'' she said, trying desperately to stop her teeth from chattering. ''But we both know the high price that riding bulls can cost.'' The feel of his warm chest pressed to her cheek and the steady beat of his heart should have been reassuring, but her fears were too strong and ran too deep.

''Honey, I love you and Amber and I want you both with me,'' he said, rubbing his hands soothingly up and down her spine. ''It's important to me for you to be there with me.'' He kissed the top of her head. ''Besides, you won't be alone. Morgan, Samantha and Annie will be sitting in the stands with you, and Brant will be down in the arena with me.''

Tears ran down her cheeks as she pulled from his arms and started to back out of the room. ''Colt, don't you understand? It doesn't matter who's with me or how many people there are around me, they couldn't stop something from happening to you.''

''Kaylee, honey, wait—''

''No.'' She stood in the doorway, her knees feeling as if they were going to buckle at any moment. ''You've always been, and will always be, my biggest weakness, Colt. I love you more than you'll ever know. But I can't watch you ride.'' She took a deep breath, then rushed on before she had a chance to change her mind. "Your shoulder is healed now, and you really don't need me—"

"I'll always need you, Kaylee," he said, taking a step toward her.

"I told you I would help you regain the use of your arm," she said quietly. "And I've done that. But I also told you I wouldn't help you get ready for the finals."

"Kaylee, don't do this," he said, taking another step toward her.

She could tell by his expression that he'd anticipated what she was about to say next. But she couldn't let that sway her. Her survival depended on it.

"Amber and I will be leaving tomorrow to go back to Oklahoma City. I'll get Annie or Samantha to drive me down to Laramie to catch a commuter flight to Denver."

Before he could respond, she turned and walked down the hall to the room she'd shared with Amber. She knew she was being a coward. But she really didn't have a choice.

She would be devastated if something tragic happened to Colt at any time. But Kaylee knew for certain that if she had to witness him being fatally injured the way she had Mitch, she'd never be able to survive. And surviving was something she had to do at all costs.

She had a little girl to think of now. Amber was depending on her. And Kaylee wasn't about to let Amber down.

Colt stood behind the bucking chutes as the bulls were being loaded into the enclosures on the last day of the Professional Bull Riders championship. He'd had an exceptional finals and was currently tied with another rider to win the season title.

But even if he achieved his goal and won the damn championship, he knew for certain the victory would be a hollow one. Hell, his whole life had been nothing but an empty void for the past two weeks—ever since Kaylee and Amber had gone back to Oklahoma.

"You ready to go out there and kick Kamikaze's butt once and for all?" Brant asked, referring to the bull Colt had never been able to ride.

Colt shrugged as he buckled his bat-wing chaps. "It's just another ride."

Dressed in the new bullfighter's uniform of shorts and matching jersey instead of the traditional baggy garb and face paint he normally wore, Brant rotated his shoulders to stay loose. "Just keep your head out there, little brother. You can take off for Oklahoma City tomorrow morning to see if you can straighten things out with Kaylee."

"What makes you think I'll be going to Oklahoma?" Colt asked, pulling on his riding glove.

"Two reasons," Brant said, sounding so certain that Colt felt like belting him one.

"What would those be?" he asked, knowing his brother would tell him anyway.

"Number one, you've been like a bear with a sore paw ever since Kaylee left. You might as well give it up and admit that nothing is more important than being with the woman you love," Brant said, bending to adjust his knee pads. When he straightened to his full height, he wore a knowing expression. "Take it from me, bro, if you don't come to that conclusion your mood is only going to get worse."

"Since when did you become an expert on affairs of the heart?" Colt asked sourly.

Brant grinned. "If you'll remember, I went through something similar with Annie before I came to my senses. I was one miserable SOB until I decided there was nothing more important than being with her."

Colt glared at his brother. "That was different. You had some stupid idea that you and Annie didn't have anything in common."

Brant grinned and went on as if Colt hadn't said anything. "And the second reason I know you'll be going to Oklahoma City is because if you don't go on your own, Morgan and I are going to stuff you on the plane ourselves."

Before Colt could respond, Brant turned and jogged out into the arena.

As Colt watched his brother take his place in front of the bucking chutes, he thought about what Brant had said. He was miserable without Kaylee and Amber. They were his life, and a hell of a lot more important than riding two thousand pounds of pissed-off beef.

He shook his head. Kaylee had told him a bull rider was who he was, and he'd pretty much agreed with her. But they'd both been wrong. There was a hell of a lot more to him than that.

Instead of looking at winning a championship buckle to define who he was, he should have considered what else he had going for him. He was a damned good rancher, the father of a precious little girl, and the man who loved Kaylee Simpson with all of his heart and soul.

Climbing the steps behind the chutes, Colt gazed down at the back of his old nemesis Kamikaze. He'd drawn the brindle bull many times in the past several years, and so far, the score was Kamikaze three, Colt zero. In fact, the bull had been the one Colt had been bucked off of the night he'd broken his collarbone.

"As far as I'm concerned, we might as well make it four to zero," Colt said, deciding that riding bulls wasn't worth losing Kaylee. "Hey, Jim?"

"What's that, hotshot?" Jim Elliott, the timekeeper asked.

"I'm not going to—"

"Colt," a familiar female voice called from somewhere behind him.

He stopped short of telling the man that he wouldn't be riding Kamikaze. Turning, he scanned the crowd of people milling around behind the chutes. Just when he thought he'd imagined hearing her, he spotted Kaylee and Amber standing not twenty feet away.

Afraid he might be hallucinating, he jumped down from the platform and rushed over to wrap his arms around them. "What are you doing here, honey?"

"Daddy," Amber said, poking her little finger into his protective black leather vest.

"That's right, little pixie," he said, kissing her baby-soft cheek.

"I couldn't stay away," Kaylee said, hugging him back. "If something happened and I wasn't with you, I don't think I could live with myself."

He shook his head as he gazed down into her pretty violet eyes. "It's no longer an issue," he said, brushing his lips over hers, then kissing the top of Amber's head. He couldn't get enough of holding them, of letting them know how much he loved them. "I was just getting ready to tell Jim that I'm turning out. I'm not going to ride Kamikaze."

She looked confused. "Why would you do that?"

"Because I love you," he said honestly. "You

and Amber mean more to me than anything else and I know it upsets you to think about me riding.''

"Colt, I love you, too." She gave him a kiss that damned near knocked him to his knees, then shook her head. ''I can't believe I'm going to say this, but I don't want you to turn out. I want you to ride that bull.''

It was his turn to look incredulous. ''What made you change your mind, honey?''

''I want you to ride because I love you and I don't ever want you to have any regrets.'' She shook her head. ''I don't want you to wonder if you could have won the championship if you'd only taken this ride.''

''Wakefield, you're up next,'' Jim called.

Colt held up his hand. ''Just a minute, Jim.'' Turning back to Kaylee, he searched her face. ''Are you sure, honey? Say the word, and I'll take the turn-out.''

He watched her take a deep breath, then meet his questioning gaze head-on. ''Yes, Colt. If Mitch were here right now, he'd kick your buns if he heard you were about to turn down a bull you could win it all on.''

''Last call, Wakefield,'' Jim shouted above the noisy crowd.

Colt stared at Kaylee for a moment longer, then, pressing his lips to hers, he smiled. ''I'll be right back, honey.''

He took the steps to the raised platform behind the bucking chutes two at a time, then stepped over the side of the tubular steel enclosure. Slipping his mouth guard into place to protect his teeth during the jarring ride, he settled himself onto the brindle bull's broad back and put his gloved hand, palm up, into the bull rope's grip.

Kamikaze tensed beneath him in anticipation of making Colt sorry he'd ever been born, but he ignored the animal's building rage. As he and some of the other riders pulled the flat braided rope snug around the bull's thick body, he was more determined than ever to keep himself from being hurt or worse. Kaylee was counting on him, and he'd go through hell and back before he let her down.

Once Colt was satisfied that the binding was as tight as it was going to get, he placed the long end of the rope in his palm and wound it around his hand several times, effectively tying himself to Kamikaze's back. Closing his fingers into a fist around the wrap, he pushed his Resistol down on his head with his free hand, took a deep breath and gave a quick nod to signal that he was ready for the ride to begin. Just as he expected, when the gate swung wide, Kamikaze exploded from the chute and out into the arena with all the energy of a keg of dynamite.

With his left arm extended above his head for balance, he gripped the animal's sides with his thighs and concentrated on staying with the bull jump for jump. True to style, Kamikaze took two high leaps, then circled to the left and settled into a tight, bucking spin.

Every lurching move of the two thousand pounds of pure fury pulled mercilessly on his right arm and made Colt feel as if someone had lifted him high into the air then slammed him down with the force of a wrecking ball. Directing all of his energy toward hanging on to the rope and keeping his body aligned with the center of the bull's back, Colt tried to anticipate Kamikaze's next move.

Adrenaline raced through his veins as he focused on every nuance of the ride and he knew the moment the eight-second whistle blew that he'd finally bested his nemesis. Reaching down between his legs, he released his hand from the bull rope and jumped clear of the angry animal.

Kaylee clutched Amber and held her breath as she watched Colt successfully ride Kamikaze. She prayed that he wouldn't hang up in the rope or fall as he landed on the dirt floor of the arena when it came time for his dismount. But to her relief, Colt managed to stay on his feet and sprint to safety, while Brant and the other two bullfighters distracted the big, ugly bull.

Watching Brant wrap Colt in a congratulatory bear hug, then seeing the ear-to-ear grin on his face, she knew she'd made the right choice in coming to the finals. She'd spent two agonizing weeks vacillating between staying in Oklahoma City or being at his side. And in the end, she'd known that she really never had any choice in the matter. When you loved someone as much as she loved Colt, you simply accepted that person and didn't try to change them.

She wasn't sure how she was going to manage watching Colt climb on the back of a bull every weekend for the next several years, knowing that at any time something could go terribly wrong. But in the past two weeks she had quickly reached the conclusion that living with the fear was something she was going to have to get used to. It couldn't be worse than the debilitating loneliness of living without him in her life at all.

"Daddy," Amber said, holding her arms out to Colt when he slipped through the arena gate and made his way to them through the crowd of well-wishers.

Happy for him, Kaylee's eyes filled with moisture as he lifted Amber to sit on his forearm, then put his other arm around her shoulders. "You did it, Colt. You won."

Still grinning, he nodded. "I guess I did." When a tear slipped down her cheek, Colt's smile disappeared instantly as he wiped it away with his finger. "Honey, are you all right?"

She nodded. "I'm just happy you won and relieved you're all right."

"Kaylee, there's something I want to tell you—" At the sound of his name being announced over the loudspeaker, he smiled apologetically. "Dang, I need to—"

Reaching up to kiss his lean cheek, she smiled and reached for Amber. "Go accept your award. You've earned it. We'll be right here waiting for you."

"Honey, you don't know how good that sounds to me." He gave her a quick kiss, then turned and walked back out into the arena for the presentation of the trophies.

Kaylee listened as the announcer presented the championship cup and an oversize check to the bull rider who had the most points for the season. The cowboy thanked the good Lord above for blessing him with an injury-free season and the fans for their support. Then the announcer turned to Colt and handed him a big gold buckle and a check for a huge amount of money for winning the finals. Colt thanked everyone, then asked the man holding the microphone if he could make an announcement.

"Well, sure...I guess that would be okay," the man said, wearing a bewildered expression.

"I've had a great career with the PBR," Colt said, his voice booming across the now eerily quiet arena. "And I couldn't have asked for this season to have ended any better." Kaylee watched Colt take a deep breath. "That's why I'm going out a winner. It's time to hang up my chaps and spurs and join the ranks of the retired."

The crowd seemed to emit a collective gasp a moment before they gave him a standing ovation.

Tears blurred Kaylee's vision. Colt was giving up his career as a bull rider. He was no longer going to tempt fate.

By the time he pushed his way through the crowd and made it back to her, she couldn't stop trembling. "Why Colt?"

Smiling, he hugged her and Amber. "Because you two are more important to me than anything else."

She shook her head. "Please don't quit because of me," she said, shaking her head. "I don't want you having any regrets."

"I don't, honey." He took Amber from her, then draped his arm across her shoulders and started walking toward the staging area behind the bucking chutes. "I've won the finals and made a good showing every year since I joined the PBR. I have nothing left to prove to anyone, but how much I love you and our daughter." He bent his head to kiss her cheek. "Besides, I don't want to be so banged up that I miss one night of making love with you for the rest of my life."

Kaylee's heart skipped a beat. "For the rest of your life?"

"Yep." When he stopped walking and turned to face her, the love she saw shining in his incredible blue eyes stole her breath. "Will you do me the honor of being my wife, Kaylee Simpson? Will you live with me on the Lonetree Ranch, allow me to be a full-time daddy to Amber and let me give you more babies?"

"Y-yes," Kaylee said, closing her eyes to the light-headed feeling sweeping over her.

"Honey, are you okay?" Colt asked, taking hold of her arm to support her.

"I seem to get kind of woozy when I get excited lately," she said, frowning. "The only other time I was like this was when I got pregnant with…" Her voice trailed off as she stared up at the man she'd loved all of her life.

"The whirlpool," he said, grinning. He pulled her forward and kissed her until her head swam.

"Daddy, Mommy," Amber said, wrapping her little arms around both of their necks.

"Would you like a new baby brother or sister, little pixie?" Colt asked.

"Yes," Amber said, nodding her head affirmatively.

"Hey, she got it right," he said, laughing. His expression suddenly turned serious. "Kaylee, how do you feel about having another baby?"

Smiling, she gazed up at the man and child she loved with all her heart. "I'd love to have another baby with raven hair and Wakefield blue eyes."

His grin returned. "Let's go find a chapel and make it official."

"No," she said, shaking her head.

"What do you mean, no?" he asked, looking as if that was the last thing he'd expected her to say. "No, you've changed your mind and you don't want to marry me? Or, no you don't want to get married in Vegas?"

She reached up to smooth the frown marring his forehead. "No, I don't want to get married in Las Vegas. If you don't mind, I'd like to have our wedding at the Lonetree. That's where we'll live, and where I'd like to start our life together."

"I like the sound of that, honey." He brushed his lips over hers. "I love you, Kaylee."

"And I love you, cowboy. More than you'll ever know."

Epilogue

Christmas Eve

"**I** feel like I'm about to choke to death," Colt said, tugging at the collar of his dress shirt.

Brant chuckled. "You're just being paid back for making fun of me and Morgan when we stood at the bottom of these stairs a few years back, waiting for our brides."

"What could be taking so long?" Colt asked, ready to climb the steps and escort Kaylee downstairs himself.

"It's my guess Annie and Samantha are fussing

over Kaylee's dress, or her hair, or anything else they can think of to fuss over." Brant shrugged. "Once you're married awhile, you'll come to realize that women like to make a fuss over the least little detail."

"They should have had plenty of time to get things ready," Colt said, frowning.

Annie and Samantha had insisted that Kaylee and Amber spend last night at the homestead with them, while Colt, Brant, Morgan and his nephews spent the night at Colt's. They'd said it was necessary because the groom wasn't supposed to see the bride until she walked down the aisle. He didn't know anything about that kind of wedding protocol, he just missed the hell out of Kaylee and couldn't wait to see her again.

When Samantha appeared at the top of the stairs, holding Amber's hand, Colt smiled. His daughter looked like a little pixie in her red-velvet-and-white-lace dress.

"Daddy," she said, pointing to him as Samantha helped her down the steps. Once they got to the bottom she held up her arms for him to pick her up. "Up, Daddy. Up."

Without hesitation, Colt bent and swung her up to sit on his forearm. It thrilled Colt at how fast Amber had become a Daddy's girl.

"Are you ready to help Mommy and Daddy get married?" he asked, kissing her cheek.

Nodding, she smiled. "Yes."

"Get ready, little brother," Brant said when Annie walked across the loft area and stopped at the top of the stairs. "You're about to join the ranks of the blissfully hitched."

Colt grinned. "I never in a million years thought I'd ever say this, but it can't be soon enough for me."

Samantha turned on the CD player, and as she herded his nephews over to stand by the large Christmas tree on the other side of the fireplace, the country group Lonestar's lead singer began to sing about being amazed by the woman he loved. Watching Annie descend the stairs, Colt waited until Brant offered his arm, then escorted her over to stand in front of the big stone fireplace where Preacher Hill from the Methodist church down in Bear Creek stood, waiting to perform the marriage ceremony.

"Mommy pitty," Amber said suddenly, pointing to the loft.

When he glanced up, Colt sucked in a sharp breath. Kaylee stood at the top of the stairs, her hand tucked in the crook of Morgan's arm. Dressed in a white satin-and-lace wedding gown, her shiny auburn hair piled in soft curls on top of her head, she was absolutely beautiful.

"Yes, Amber," Colt said, stepping forward. "Your mommy is the prettiest woman I've ever seen."

At the bottom of the steps, Morgan smiled and placed Kaylee's hand in Colt's. He kissed Kaylee's cheek, then patted Colt on the shoulder.

"Take good care of each other," he said, then took his place with Samantha and the boys by the Christmas tree.

"Are you ready to become Mrs. Colt Wakefield?" he asked, grinning.

The smile Kaylee gave him sent his temperature sky-high. "I've been ready for this moment all of my life."

Colt grinned. "So have I, honey. I just didn't realize it."

With Kaylee on one arm and Amber in the other, Colt walked them over to the big stone fireplace for Preacher Hill to make their union complete.

Three hours later, after putting Amber to bed upstairs, Kaylee and Colt sat on the couch in their living room, holding each other. A cozy fire blazed in the fireplace, but other than the twinkling lights on the Christmas tree, the room was romantically dim.

"Colt?"

"What, honey?"

"I have an early Christmas present for you," she said, rising to retrieve a brightly wrapped box from beneath the tree.

"But I thought we were going to wait until tomorrow morning to exchange presents,'' Colt said, frowning.

Kaylee shook her head. ''I'd rather give this to you now.''

She nibbled on her lower lip as he turned the box over in his hands then shook it. ''It's pretty light,'' he said, grinning. When he tore the wrapping away and lifted the box lid, he frowned. ''What's this?''

''That's a copy of the ultrasound,'' she said, unable to stop smiling. ''You know I had my second prenatal check yesterday.''

Until the wedding, they hadn't seen each other since she, Annie and Samantha had returned from Laramie the afternoon before. And news like this just couldn't be shared over the phone.

''What did the doctor have to say?'' Colt asked, frowning as he gazed at the paper in his hand. ''Is everything all right?''

Grinning, she reached up to smooth the frown from his brow with her fingertips, then pointed to the picture. ''He said I'm as healthy as a horse. And so are the…babies.''

''That's a re—'' He stopped short. ''What do you mean *babies?*''

Kaylee laughed at his shocked expression. ''The doctor did this early ultrasound because he said I was getting pretty big for only being a couple of months along.'' She kissed his firm male lips. ''We're having twins, cowboy.''

A slow grin began to spread across his handsome face as he took her hand in his and kissed the wedding band on the third finger of her left hand. "Besides getting married, this is the best Christmas present I've ever received."

They held each other for some time before Colt spoke again. "If the twins are boys, would you mind if we named one of them Mitch?"

Tears filled her eyes at Colt's thoughtfulness. "I'd like that." She raised her head from his shoulder to gaze up at him. "I love you, Colt."

"And I love you, honey."

"I think this is the best Christmas ever," Kaylee said, snuggling closer.

"It's just the first of many special days, honey." Colt gave her a kiss that turned her insides to warm pudding, then stood and, smiling, held out his hand to help her up from the couch. "Now, let's go upstairs and let me show you how special the nights are going to be."

Without hesitation Kaylee put her hand in his, anxious to start their lives together as man and wife on their part of the Lonetree Ranch.

*   *   *   *   *

Don't miss Kathie DeNosky's next book,
REMEMBERING ONE WILD NIGHT,
available from Silhouette Desire
in January 2004.

Silhouette® Desire®

is proud to present
an exciting new miniseries from

KATHIE DeNOSKY

Lonetree Ranchers

On the Lonetree Ranch, passions explode
under Western skies for these
handsome-but-hard-to-tame bachelors.

In August 2003—
LONETREE RANCHERS: BRANT

In October 2003—
LONETREE RANCHERS: MORGAN

In December 2003—
LONETREE RANCHERS: COLT

Available at your favorite retail outlet.

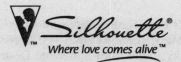

Silhouette®
Where love comes alive™

Silhouette Desire

TEXAS Cattleman's Club

The Stolen Baby

Silhouette Desire's powerful miniseries features
six wealthy Texas bachelors—all members of
the state's most prestigious club—who set out
to unravel the mystery surrounding one tiny
baby...and discover true love in the process!

This newest installment
continues with,

Remembering One Wild Night

by KATHIE DeNOSKY

(Silhouette Desire #1559)

Meet Travis Whelan—a jet-setting attorney...
and a *father?* When Natalie Perez showed up
in his life again with the baby daughter he'd
never known about, Travis knew he had
a duty to both of them. But could he
find a way to make them a family?

Available January 2004 at your favorite retail outlet.

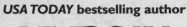

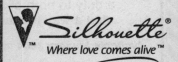

January 2004

A brand-new
family saga begins.

DYNASTIES : THE DANFORTHS

A family of prominence...
tested by scandal,
sustained by passion!

Become immersed in the lives of
the Danforths and enter the
high-powered world of Savannah society.
Danforth patriarch Abraham Danforth's
surprising decision to run for state Senate
will unleash a chain of events uncovering
long-hidden secrets, testing this family
more than they ever imagined.

Available at your favorite retail outlet.

COMING NEXT MONTH

#1555 THE CINDERELLA SCANDAL—Barbara McCauley
Dynasties: The Danforths
Tina Alexander had always lived in the shadows of her gorgeous sisters,
so imagine her surprise when Reid Danforth walked into her family bakery
with heated gazes aimed only at her! Soon the two fell into bed—and into
an unexpected relationship. But would this Cinderella's hidden scandal put
an end to their fairy-tale romance?

#1556 FULL THROTTLE—Merline Lovelace
To Protect and Defend
Paired together for a top secret test mission, scientist Kate Hargrave and
U.S. Air Force Captain Dave Scott clashed from the moment they met, setting
off sparks with every conflict. Would it be only a matter of time before Kate
gave in to Dave's advances…and discovered a physical attraction neither
would know how to walk away from?

#1557 MIDNIGHT SEDUCTION—Justine Davis
Redstone, Incorporated
An inheritance and a cryptic note led Emma Purcell to the Pacific
Northwest—and to sexy Harlen McClaren. As Emma and Harlen unraveled
the mystery left behind by her late cousin, pent-up passions came to life,
taking over their senses…and embedding them in the deepest mystery of
all: love!

#1558 LET IT RIDE—Katherine Garbera
King of Hearts
Vacationing in Vegas was exactly what Kylie Smith needed. The lights! The
casinos! The quickie marriages? Billionaire casino owner Deacon Prescott
spotted Kylie on the security monitor and knew the picture of domesticity
would be perfect as his wife: Prim in public, passionate in private. But was
Deacon prepared to get more than he bargained for?

#1559 REMEMBERING ONE WILD NIGHT—Kathie DeNosky
Texas Cattleman's Club: The Stolen Baby
Waking from amnesia, single mother Natalie Perez knew her child was
in danger. High-powered lawyer Travis Whelan was the only man who could
protect her daughter—the man who had lied to her and broken her heart…and
the father of her baby. Would the wild attraction they shared overcome past
betrayals and unite them as a family?

#1560 AT YOUR SERVICE—Amy Jo Cousins
Runaway heiress Grace Haley donned an apron and posed as a
waitress while trying to get out from under her powerful—and manipulative—
family's thumb. Grace just wanted a chance to figure out her life. Instead she
found herself sparring with her boss, sexy pub owner Christopher Tyler, and
soon her hands were full of more than just dishes.…